# ROYAL COURTSHIP

# Royal Courtship

*by*
Livvy West

**Dales Large Print Books**
Long Preston, North Yorkshire,
England.

British Library Cataloguing in Publication Data.

West, Livvy
 Royal courtship.

A catalogue record for this book is
available from the British Library

ISBN 1-85389-587-3 pbk

First published in Great Britain by D.C. Thomson & Co.,
Ltd., 1994

Copyright © 1994 by Livvy West

Published in Large Print September 1995 by arrangement
with Marina Oliver.

Dales Large Print is an imprint of
Library Magna Books Ltd.
Printed and bound in Great Britain by
T.J. Press (Padstow) Ltd., Cornwall, PL28 8RW.

# CHAPTER 1

'Would that I could dance with you, Mistress Davenport! But I fear—this leg of mine is troublesome. I shall give myself the pleasure of watching, however, the loveliest young lady at Court. Now let me see—boy!'

Isabella Davenport gave way to treasonable thoughts. What horrid misfortune was it that had brought her to the notice of this gross mountain of a man now sitting on the throne of England?

King Henry was, luckily for Bella, unaware of her opinion, or the glance of desperation she cast towards a dark, olive-skinned, raven-haired man standing a few feet away.

'More music!' the King called, then turned back to her. 'After you have danced the measure, I will talk with you. I would know you better, Mistress Bella.'

7

If a king could be said to leer, Bella thought, Henry Tudor was a champion, as he had in his youth been a champion in the tournaments and jousts.

'As you will, my lord,' she murmured submissively.

There were a few moments of silence, during which the King smiled complacently at Bella, and she willed herself not to reveal her fear and hatred. When she thought she could bear it no longer, the King grunted in satisfaction.

'My dear, you will dance with the Comte de Nerac. Charles, I know I can depend on you to take care of the lovely Mistress Davenport. I shall be watching with interest.'

Bella raised her eyes to the man bowing before her, and drew in her breath swiftly and almost forgot the peril she stood in because of the King's interest. He was a stranger, she had never before seen him, but in a court overflowing with handsome, young men he was outstanding.

Tall above the average, as dark haired as she was auburn, his eyes were almost black. He sported a small, black beard, and wore a piratical jewel, a brilliant sapphire, in one ear. His doublet was of the same blue, the sleeves narrowing at the wrist, and the trunk hose slashed with a deeper shade of velvet.

There was a slight smile on his lips—firm, determined, red lips, Bella saw, as he took her hand and led her out on to the floor where a set was forming.

'I believe the King feels that our costumes match,' he said softly, and Bella realised her gown of rich, blue satin was indeed the same shade as his hose.

His voice was deep, and there was a slight, French accent.

'About as good a reason for constraining two people to dance together as any other, I suppose,' she replied sharply, and then gasped as he gripped her hand tightly.

'If you prefer not to dance with me, Mistress Davenport,' he said, 'we need not. I will make our excuses to the King so that he will blame me, not you. But I would be exceedingly sorry. I've been wondering for an hour past what pretext I could employ to become acquainted with the most beautiful girl in the room.'

Bella frowned impatiently. Why did men keep talking about beauty, when it was but a snare, an unsought device to enslave a king? Many times these last few days she'd wished with all her heart she had been born ugly and misshapen.

'I could wish I were plain and marked with the smallpox,' she murmured now under her breath, and then glanced guiltily up at the Comte as his fingers tightened on hers. Had he heard her, she wondered in sudden confusion.

But he was not looking at her, and she relaxed, letting her thoughts return to ponder on whether ugliness would have saved her the King's attentions.

Even the ill-favoured Anne of Cleves, rejected by a capricious Henry when the reality did not match the flattering portrait Mr Holbein had made of her, was not concerned. Plain as she was, she worried that the King might be turning his eyes towards her again.

He had been heard to proclaim his desire

for an older, more sensible wife. If his fancy alighted on his 'good sister,' as he called her, she would have to abandon her happy retirement.

For some time now the King, with only the sickly Prince Edward as his acknowledged heir, had been searching for yet another wife and more sons. Both his daughters had been declared illegitimate, although Mary had been restored to the succession, but in any case no queen had ever reigned on England's throne.

The ladies of his Court, as well as European princesses, were wary. They remembered the two discarded wives, the one dead in childbed, and most of all, the two Henry had called traitors and beheaded.

Besides, Henry was an unattractive bridegroom. He was no longer the handsome, vibrant Prince who rode and hunted and danced better than other men. He was old, fat, ill and hasty tempered. Even the prospect of an influence on political matters did not outweigh the disadvantages of such a marriage.

Bella's musings were interrupted as the Comte spoke.

'I have not seen you at Court before,' he was saying.

'I have only recently arrived. I am with the Lady Mary's household,' Bella explained. 'You, my lord, are French?'

'I am.'

He said no more of his reason for being there, but Bella was well aware that negotiations had been started for a marriage between her mistress, the Lady Mary, the King's eldest daughter, and Charles of Orleans, a younger son of the French King Francis. The Comte must be attached to the French embassy.

Instead he talked easily of the magnificent palace, the paintings and tapestries which now adorned it, and the journey up-river from London he had made some days before.

He spoke so interestingly Bella almost forgot the apprehension which gripped her. When the dance finished and he led her back to the stool beside Henry, she recalled with a frisson of fear that now she would be obliged to smile sweetly at her liege lord and agree dutifully with his remarks.

Once more she glanced towards the dark-haired man, but he was talking animatedly to a small group of courtiers, and did not look in her direction. Bella sighed, but recognised his wisdom. If he gave her sign of their attachment the King would wreak some revenge. No man dared poach on royal preserves.

At last the King grew tired and went to bed. Bella, once she was certain he had gone, moved slowly down the room, exchanging a word here and there with others until she reached the group round the dark-haired man.

'You look as beautiful as ever, cousin,' he said and smiled at her in the way that made her tremble with excitement.

'The King agrees with you, Pedro,' another of the group commented. 'Are we soon to have a Queen Isabella?'

Bella shuddered, and another girl put a comforting arm about her shoulders.

'It would sound rude if I said he would soon lose interest,' she said with a laugh, 'but I sincerely hope he does, Bella!'

'Indeed, Amy, so do I!' another girl said suddenly, and Bella glanced over her shoulder. The King's daughter was taking the first opportunity to depart for her own rooms now that her royal father was gone, and as women of the bedchamber, attending the Lady Mary, Bella and Amy must accompany her.

As they turned to follow, Pedro grasped Bella's hand and held her back.

'Tomorrow morning, the usual place?' he murmured softly, and she nodded, smiled tremulously, and as he released her turned away to rejoin Amy.

Unaccustomed to Court life, the King's oldest daughter was drooping with fatigue. She spoke little as her ladies prepared her for bed, and finally Bella escaped to her own small room which she and Amy shared.

'Bella, do not look so miserable,' Amy said as they prepared for bed. 'You do not really think the King will want to marry you, do you?'

'I pray not, but I am afraid!' Bella

replied, as she untied the strings of her petticoats.

'If he does mean it, you shall have to run away with Pedro.'

'Pedro? But, Amy, what—'

Amy broke in impatiently. 'Do not pretend, Bella! He is your cousin, he is rich and handsome, and he shows a decided preference for you. It would not be strange if you were a little in love with him!'

Confused, Bella turned away to hide her burning cheeks.

'I like him,' she admitted slowly, 'but I am not at all sure I love him. How can one tell?'

'When you fall in love, you will not have to ask anyone else's opinion about your feelings,' Amy said slowly, and Bella turned to glance at her friend.

Amy was unusually serious, and for a second Bella caught a look of pain and despair on her friend's face. This was so odd for the carefree Amy that she did not know what to say, and was thankful when Amy blew out the candle and wished her a sleepy, 'Good-night.'

Bella's sleep was far from peaceful. There was the puzzle of Amy's unexpected unhappiness to keep her awake, for never before had she suspected that her friend was in love, and, it seemed, hopelessly. After she finally slept, images of Henry and Pedro and the Comte de Nerac whirled about her dreams, and when she rose and slipped from the room without waking Amy, she was heavy-eyed. Her step was light, however, for she was going to meet Pedro, and they would steal a few precious moments together.

Pedro was waiting for her in a secluded spot near the river, and pulled her to him possessively, kissing her hungrily.

'I do not know how I refrained from murdering that obscene lump of lard last night,' he murmured into her hair. 'I wanted to kill that vain Frenchman, too, when he was commanded to dance with you and all I could do was watch and be jealous that it was he, not I, holding your hand.'

Bella laughed a trifle breathlessly. Pedro's fierce declarations when they were alone both thrilled and frightened her. No-one else affected her in this way, no-one else seemed so passionately resentful if another man paid attention to her. Yet she had met him, this Spanish cousin, only a week ago, and in her innermost being she doubted whether anyone could fall in love so suddenly as it appeared Pedro had.

'Let us walk along the riverbank,' she suggested. Pedro took her arm and they turned away from the palace. 'The Comte was only doing as the King commanded,' she said lightly. 'I mean nothing to him, but I am afraid of Henry!'

'You do not wish to be Queen?' Pedro demanded.

'Of course not! Who could possibly want to be married to an old man with a reputation for killing off his wives?' she demanded indignantly. 'They still speak of it, those who were here,' she went on, shuddering. 'Some say they can still hear poor Catherine Howard's screams as she ran along the gallery and tried to get to the King to plead with him for mercy while he was in the chapel. He did not hear, and they dragged her back to her apartments. Within months she was dead! No other lady wishes to end up on the block at Tower Green!'

'Don't worry,' Pedro said reassuringly. 'If the King grows more serious we will flee to Spain, you and I. He cannot follow us there, and we will live safely and happily ever after.'

Bella nodded, but the prospect of leaving her own country and facing life in Spain dismayed her a little. It was her mother's country, and she would be with Pedro, but she loved her home in the gentle, rolling hills of the Cotswolds, and she had heard disturbing accounts of the rigid, Spanish etiquette.

Henry's Court was not nearly so stiff and formal, and at home she was given a great deal of freedom, for her brother was away at Court and her grandmother old and indulgent.

Pedro was speaking again.

'I have to leave early this morning, to go back to London. I will return in a week or so, but I had to say a private farewell to my lovely Bella! Remember you are mine, and no-one else, not even the great King Henry, shall have you! Now kiss me, pretty cousin! Give me a token I can remember while I am engaged in tedious business in London.'

After he left in the barge which was to take him down-river to London, Bella went to sit on a fallen tree trunk in a secluded part of the park overlooking the wide, smooth bend in the river. Perhaps the fresh air would dispel the sluggishness she felt after a disturbed night, and help resolve her tumultuous thoughts.

She was unsure whether dreams of the fearful fate which awaited Henry's next bride, the prospect of life far away in a strange country, even though it would be with Pedro, who loved her, or insistent memories of the Comte's handsome face and musical voice troubled her most.

She was not left long for peaceful contemplation.

'Bella! What are you doing here? I have searched the entire palace for you!'

'I trust you did not invade the King's

private apartments!' Bella retorted, turning with a sigh to face the man walking rapidly towards her.

He was tall and slender, with reddish hair, handsome in a gentle, most effeminate way.

He ignored her bitterness and a gratified smile kept appearing on his face as he talked.

'Bella, the King is enchanted with you! He was talking about you last night and again this morning. He was praising both your beauty and your good sense.'

'Since it would be rather obvious if I were to disfigure myself, I shall have to indulge in foolishness!'

'Bella, my dear sister, you must not be frightened. Think what a marvellous chance it would be to our family if the King favoured you!'

'Surely you could not agree?' she whispered, aghast.

'How could either of us object?' he replied impatiently. 'We have to do as the King commands, but you may be sure I will obtain the best bargain I can, and if by some misfortune Henry insists on waiting to see whether you are prompt to conceive, I will be in a good position to demand a very good settlement.'

For a moment Bella was speechless, then she leaped to her feet and burst into a furious tirade.

'So, Thomas. You propose to sell me to the King as his paramour? I thought even you would have more pride, more sense of the duty you owe to your family, the memory of our parents, than to sink to such depths! What man would want me once I had been discarded, even with your bribe?'

'Be quiet, someone might hear! You talk nonsense! Of course I would insist on marriage, if at all possible, but you must see King Henry's point of view,' he added in a persuasive tone. 'After so many disappointments he needs reassurance that any new wife will be able to give him a healthy heir.'

'Has he ever considered the possibility that he might now be incapable of fathering a child?'

21

Her brother chuckled. 'If that's the truth, there are ways of deceiving him! Catherine Howard was too indiscreet. Bella, just think what a wonderful advantage this could be for the Davenports!'

'You call false allegations and execution an advantage?' Bella demanded furiously, her voice rising. 'No, my dear Thomas, you may be ten years older than I and my guardian, but I'll never agree to marry that bloated, monstrous, crazy freak of a man—'

'Hush, you fool!' Sir Thomas Davenport cried, seizing Bella and clamping his hand over her mouth as he looked round fearfully. 'Have you no more sense than to speak treason, and get us all beheaded!'

'Rather now than after being seduced by that monster!' Bella muttered rebelliously, but quietly. She was well aware of the King's sudden, unpredictable rages. She knew many eyes and ears pried incessantly, ready to report any word or act which might advance the spy and damage the spied upon.

'Bella, be sensible,' Sir Thomas pleaded

as he spread out his cloak and pulled her down again to sit beside him on the log. 'Let us discuss this calmly. The King has taken a fancy to you, and he needs another wife. It would be the surest way to advance our family. We might become as great as the Howards and Seymours.'

'We do not have an endless supply of sacrificial brides,' Bella pointed out. 'We are alone, without influential relatives. And most of the Howards are at present in the Tower. It is so overcrowded with Howards some have to lodge in the City. I do not call that a great future, even were I to escape the block!'

For some time he argued, but she was firm in her refusal to do anything to promote herself in the King's favour.

'I mean to ask the Lady Mary if I may be excused. I wish to go to Grandmother's.'

'He cannot live long, they say,' her brother continued, ignoring her.

'Thomas, that's far worse treason than anything I've said! You know he cannot abide any mention of his death. I suppose he imagines he's immortal.'

'It might be for just a few years, a few months,' Thomas urged.

'One day—or night—would be a lifetime in Hell!'

'You are a foolish and ungrateful wench! Here is a magnificent opportunity to advance the Davenports, and you have ridiculously childish notions! No-one marries to please themselves, Bella. It's a matter of family advancement, suitable alliances such as I was planning when Sir John Talbot proposed a marriage with you. If you hadn't had the chance to come to Court you could have been married to him by now.'

'It may be no more than a political alliance for kings, and my poor Lady Mary who has been promised to so many but never had the chance of marriage. I am thankful I am not royal, for I mean to marry a man I can love and respect.'

Thomas rose. 'I shall ask Jane to speak with you.'

'She may talk all day—which is nothing unusual for your dear wife—but I will not be persuaded,' Bella declared.

Sir Thomas, with a final despairing glare at her, turned and strode away.

'Pompous, unfeeling fool!' Bella muttered, and then almost fell off the log in surprise as a deep chuckle answered her.

'Who—what?' she exclaimed, springing up in alarm. She hadn't realised before how close the log was to a thick clump of bushes. As she stared in fright, wondering whether to call for Thomas or take to her heels, the Comte de Nerac emerged and walked slowly towards her.

'I beg your pardon, Mistress Bella, but I was sitting on the far side of the bushes, and when I realised what was happening, it seemed better not to embarrass you by announcing my presence. Do please sit down again. You look white with shock.'

'Did—did you hear it all?' Bella asked, breathless with apprehension. It was all very well to express treasonable opinions in private, or to a brother who, however exasperated he might be, would never betray her. It might be fatal if this man, a Frenchman, wished to cause trouble.

He took her hands and urged her to sit

on the log beside him, retaining her hands in a comforting grasp.

'I heard enough. Do not be afraid. I won't betray you. He was your brother?'

'Yes. And as you heard, all he cares about is family advancement. His wife is even more ambitious. She is delighted Lady Mary is in favour now, welcomed at Court, but I never dreamed I might find the King so attentive to me.'

'Why not? You are very beautiful. Any man might wish to possess you, even a King.'

She could not suppress the tremble that shook her, as he tightened his grip.

'I could not! I know it is my duty to marry well, and obey my brother, but—I cannot! There is something about the King which terrifies me! I mean his person, not just the fear he might order my death with as little thought as he would trap a rabbit.'

'That is not surprising, Bella. He's old and fat and ill, and a woman as lovely as you deserves a mate more fitting. Is there a man you prefer?'

Bella gave a shaky laugh.

'Almost anyone!' she said vehemently. 'No-one I like enough to marry, although several men have asked Thomas for my hand.'

She thought of Pedro. Did she wish to marry him? She didn't know, so she was telling the truth.

'I have a good dowry, adequate rather than ample,' she continued. 'So far he hasn't considered any of them important enough, although he was tempted by an offer from a man who lives near our home, and who owns land which adjoins ours. I think he would have accepted that if I had not been given the chance to serve the Lady Mary. So I've been spared the necessity of refusing them. I cannot even escape into a nunnery like my Aunt Anne did now the King has closed them!' she added bitterly. 'But I am making too much noise. The King has merely shown his admiration for me, and he has been casting sheep's eyes at many ladies since he mur—that is, since Catherine Howard was beheaded.

I doubt he will remember me in a few days.'

'That is something to hope for,' the Comte said, but there was an odd note in his voice which disturbed Bella.

'You will not betray me, will you?' she asked shyly. 'I know it is a great deal to ask, but—'

'A great deal? To protect a lovely girl from the wrath of a spurned and ugly old lecher? You must think Frenchmen are fools or villains! Of course I will say nothing about your indiscretions. Though I could wish you might be indiscreet enough to reward me with a kiss! I am neither old nor, I trust, ugly.'

Bella laughed, but her blushes betrayed her confusion, and with a laugh the Comte rose to his feet.

'Come, it will soon be time for dinner. I will escort you back to the palace. And be content, my beautiful one, I will forget all I overheard.'

# CHAPTER 2

On the following morning, the King commanded Bella to join his riding party. It was a sedate affair, compared with Henry's early years, one of the older men, William Eames explained as they rode through the Tiltyard into the Park.

'The King is too old and heavy for the exciting chases we once enjoyed,' he said regretfully. 'You should have seen him then. None would match him for beauty and strength and courage.'

'Not even King Francis or the Emperor?' a new voice enquired.

Bella felt her cheeks burning, and dared not look up at the Comte de Nerac, who had brought his horse alongside hers. Would he read in her eyes the admission she had been thinking of him continuously since the previous day? Would he see how

29

guilty she felt at having thought so little about Pedro?

William Eames laughed. 'It was a glorious sight to see the Kings of France and England, both young and vigorous, together at the Field of the Cloth of Gold. And the Emperor with Henry, too, but that was more than twenty years since. Age attacks us all. It has some compensations. We grow wiser, ride quietly and let the young and the huntsmen do the work.'

The group of courtiers spread out across the Park. None was incautious enough to outride the King, so progress was slow. Bella nevertheless found herself enjoying this ride more than previous ones. Perhaps it was the presence of the Comte de Nerac at her side, the impression he provided of a shield from the King's unwelcome attentions.

Eames had left them to join a crony, and Bella realised the Comte had gradually edged them away from the main group.

'We could wait unseen behind these trees,' he suggested, bringing his mount to a halt.

Bella looked back at him, cheeks flushed, eyes sparkling.

'Why should we do that?'

'Do you not long for a good gallop? We could let these beasts stretch their legs. My poor mount is fidgeting as though he hasn't gone at more than a trot for years, and yours is restive, too.'

'We might not be back in time for dinner,' she said slowly. It was so tempting to escape for a while from the imposed decorum and underlying threats at Court.

'We can eat at a tavern somewhere, and make some excuse afterwards if anyone enquires. Well, Mistress Davenport, are you not willing to take a risk?'

Suddenly she decided. 'Yes! Oh, I feel like a naughty child escaping from the nursery. I shall be sent to bed without supper!'

They slipped behind the trees and watched the rest of the party vanish.

'Come. We have not been missed,' the Comte said. 'We can safely take our own way.'

They set off, in high spirits, and when

they came to an open stretch, let the horses have their heads.

'I haven't done that for years!' Bella laughed as they slowed at last.

'You were brought up in the country?' the Comte asked.

'Yes, in Oxfordshire, by my grandmother.'

'Your parents?'

'My mother died a year after I was born, and my father three years ago in a hunting accident. Grandmother is my father's mother, for my mother was Spanish.'

'Which explains the lovely brown eyes. How did she come to England?'

'With Queen Catherine of Aragon. She was one of her ladies. It was for her sake that the Lady Mary took me into her household, though now I could wish she had not.'

'It seems ungallant to say it, but perhaps the King will turn his attention to another soon.'

'I hope he does, though I pity her with all my heart!' Bella said fervently.

'Forget him, we came here to escape

the Court. Tell me more about your childhood. I have met your brother, but I understand Signor de Mendoza is your cousin.'

'Yes, his mother and mine were sisters. Pedro lived with us for a year when he was about twelve, to improve his English since he was destined for the diplomatic service. I do not recall much as I was only about three at the time.'

He was so easy to talk to, Bella found, that soon they were behaving as old friends. While she described her home in the Cotswolds he responded by telling her about his family's chateau in the Loire valley.

When their horses were tired they turned back, and the Comte led her to a small tavern on the banks of the river. He was obviously known there, and the innkeeper swiftly produced savoury tongue pie for them which was followed by apple mousse, washed down with cool ale.

They returned to the palace laughing together, conspirators, and in the following days, the Comte sought her out frequently.

Bella was surprised how quickly the time sped past, so that when Pedro returned from London and she met him in one of the galleries she greeted him with an astonished look.

'You are back soon, cousin,' she said smiling. 'I am pleased to see you.'

'I am a few days later than I said,' he replied with a sudden frown. 'You have contrived to amuse yourself while I have been away?' he asked, and then lowered his voice. 'Meet me in the usual place early tomorrow morning. I have missed you, my dear Bella.'

When she reached their trysting spot, however, she found him in a black mood. He was staring out across the river, and turned slowly when she hesitantly spoke.

'Pedro? Is all well?'

'You are faithless, so how can all be well with me?' he replied. 'When you were surprised at seeing me yesterday I suspected something was wrong.'

'Faithless? What can be wrong? I do not understand. Surely you cannot think I am reconciled to the King's attentions?'

34

she replied indignantly.

'Not the King, no. I have heard much about your infatuation with the handsome Frenchman. It is the talk of the Court, and I am surprised the King has not heard of it. He will be furious when he does.'

'There is nothing to hear! Am I to ignore everyone else at Court just because the King pays me attentions!'

'You spurn a crown, but perhaps being a French countess is better than marrying a Spanish cousin, a younger son with no prospect of inheriting my father's title!'

'I am not infatuated with anyone!' she declared, her cheeks burning and her eyes flashing. She tried to hold on to her fiery temper and speak reasonably. 'If you mean the Comte de Nerac, he is kind, and we can talk together easily,' she tried to explain.

'Talk? You must think me gullible if you wish me to believe that is all you do!' he retorted.

'It is, Pedro. I cannot complain to any Englishman about the King, for fear they will betray me, but the Comte owes him no loyalty and seeks no favours. He is sympathetic. But there is nothing else, I swear. He has no more thought of marrying me than I have of marrying the King!'

'Then marry me! Let us announce our betrothal, and it will put an end to the King's importunity.'

'Marry you?' she said slowly. 'I—I have not thought of it.'

'But we know one another well, do we not, and what could be more fitting? Thomas would agree, and you would be in no more danger from the King.'

'Henry would be furious,' she replied, and shivered with apprehension. 'Even if he has no intention of marrying me himself, he would be angry with us all. And Thomas grows more certain every day that his attentions are becoming most marked. If I appeared to spurn him by becoming betrothed to someone else I would be banished from Court—'

'You would leave in any case to live with me, and he cannot punish me. We can go straight to Spain. Say yes, Bella. Do you not know how much I want to call you my own?'

She shook her head. 'We might escape punishment, but Thomas would be disgraced. I cannot bring that on him.'

'Thomas was willing to sell you to Henry for his own advancement,' Pedro reminded her. 'He knows young Prince Edward is not expected to live. He believes that if you had a son and Henry died, he would become Regent and rule himself. He cares so little for your happiness, why should you consider his?'

'Just because he puts ambition before my welfare does not mean I have to behave with the same lack of family regard,' Bella said slowly. 'I could not do it, Pedro. Besides, it is more than just his happiness at stake. His very life might be in danger if the King felt slighted!'

'Then you do not wish to marry me?' he asked in an offended tone.

'I do not know! Pedro, I like you. I enjoy your company, but apart from risking the King's displeasure, I do not know whether I love you!'

'Love? Women are not supposed to consider irrelevant feelings like love when a marriage is proposed. It is enough that I find you desirable, for I will make you love me. It will be our duty.'

'But until the King's interest in me declines, I cannot answer! It would be too dangerous.'

He shrugged and began to talk of his visit to London. Bella was relieved, for she genuinely did not know her true feelings. Was the excitement she felt when Pedro kissed her the sort of love she craved in a husband? She had nothing to compare it with. Her mother having died when she was a baby meant she had not experienced real, family affection, and she knew her brother Thomas had married Jane for the sake of her large dowry and her father's influence at Court. They regarded marriage as the sort of business arrangement Bella was determined to avoid, for she considered it an arid, joyless condition. She dreamed of something better for herself, and yet she doubted her ability to recognise it if it appeared.

During the next few weeks, Bella was in a ferment of emotion. The King continued to pay her lavish compliments and keep her at his side during the dancing and carousing in the Great Hall after supper, and his attentions were marked enough to cause a wave of gossip. Several times the other ladies stopped speaking abruptly as Bella entered a room, and many cast her sympathetic glances.

She knew they had no envy. They pitied her, but were also relieved that while the King was enamoured of her they might themselves be safe.

Bella was, below the surface, perturbed, however calm she tried to appear. Pedro took every opportunity to urge her to accept his offer of marriage, and when she resisted making a decision he eventually accused her of being flattered by the attentions of the Comte de Nerac.

'He has turned your head,' Pedro said angrily one morning when they were riding with the King, and he had contrived to come alongside her mare. 'You are become capricious. You are not the gentle, sensible

Bella you were a few weeks ago. The King's favour and the Comte's good looks have encouraged in you a flightiness I did not suspect.'

Angrily Bella denied it, and left him fuming. Her anger was fuelled by guilt, however, for her thoughts dwelt more on the fascinating Comte than was seemly. Every day she caught herself wondering when their next meeting would be. She grew restless if a day passed and he forbore to speak to her.

Amy saw the restlessness and at last Bella confided in her friend.

'So Pedro wishes to marry me, but I don't know if that is what I want. Surely if I loved him I would never look forward to seeing the Comte as I do? Yet I'm sure I don't love him! I just enjoy his company.'

'I don't think you do love Pedro, whatever your feelings for the Comte,' Amy said slowly. 'You would not have these doubts if you did.'

Recalling earlier remarks which had indicated Amy was in love and unhappy about it, Bella changed the topic of conversation. For some reason Amy could see no hope for achieving happiness. Probably the man was already married or betrothed, or Amy's love was not returned. It was even possible her family considered him an unsuitable match. Whatever the cause, if Amy did not wish to confide in her she could not burden her friend with her own worries. Somehow, she thought optimistically, everything would be resolved.

Early one morning, when she was walking near the bowling alley beside the Privy Orchard, the Comte joined her. Bella struggled to suppress her pleasure and reply composedly to his remarks.

'The Lady Mary looks ill,' he said after a while.

'She is unaccustomed to Court life. It wearies her,' Bella explained.

'If she marries she will have to endure it,' he replied. 'She has lived a retired life, I believe?'

'Yes, at Syon or Havering-atte-Bower mostly. But since Catherine Howard was disgraced, she has been summoned to Court. Isn't that why you are in England, for the negotiations about a marriage to Charles of Orleans?'

It was common knowledge that now the French King and Charles of Spain were once more at loggerheads both were trying to win Henry's support. The marriage of his daughter was one way of securing an alliance.

'It is being discussed,' he agreed lightly.

'The King would not arrange a marriage when she was banished from his sight.'

'Poor lady. It must be a very unsettling existence. I understand she has often been ill.'

Another time he asked about the medicines Mary was given, and gradually Bella began to wonder at his concern over her mistress's health. The possible reason for this she discovered talking to Mary's other ladies.

'King Francis doubts her ability to bear healthy children. Her mother had so many stillbirths and miscarriages, and My Lady is old at six and twenty to begin the business of childbirth.'

'Those damned French spies have been asking the most impertinent questions,' another said. 'They've approached the cooks in the Privy Kitchen, and even sunk so low as to question My Lady's laundress.'

Bella felt as though a hammer had thudded against her stomach. Was that why the Comte had sought her out? His compliments, which made her think a handsome, young man found her attractive, had after all been no more than a clandestine way of winning her confidence. He'd no doubt hoped by this stratagem to gain knowledge for his master which might, in some devious manner, be used against her own mistress.

Then her thoughts stopped with a jolt. She had been most unwise in confiding her true feelings about the King to the Comte. How did she know he might not, to curry favour with King Henry, repeat what she had said? She'd been wickedly incautious to trust him. Just because he appeared sympathetic did not mean he merited such trust.

He'd sought her out, eavesdropped on her conversation with her brother, and made himself pleasant. Was it all some devious plan? Perhaps the eavesdropping had been deliberate, not accidental after all. If so, he was despicable. It was not honourable conduct. If he could do this, what else might he do in furthering his master's plans?

He asked many questions about Lady Mary's health. He'd been more concerned than a stranger should have been. He was part of the embassy which had come from the French Court to negotiate a marriage. Of course the French would wish to discover as much as they could about the prospective bride, but they did it by underhand means.

When the Comte, after supper that day, came to speak with her, she was cold and distant.

'Are you ill, my dear Bella?' he asked in concern when she responded to all his remarks with brief, cold replies.

'You should be an apothecary, you

have so much interest in our health,' she snapped, and turned away abruptly.

After a long and thoughtful look, he turned away, and soon afterwards she saw him talking animatedly with another girl. Instead she was wretched. So distracted was she that when the King commanded her to come and sit beside him she scarcely listened to him.

'My dear little Isabella,' Henry said, squeezing her hand so hard that she gasped and dragged her attention back. 'You like my plan?'

'Plan? Sire, I beg pardon, I did not hear. What plan?' she stammered, and was aware of her brother glowering at her from the other side of the King.

'Aren't you listening?' Henry demanded, and Bella winced at the loud tones.

'I—my head pains me. I feel hot, feverish,' she murmured slowly. 'I beg pardon. What plan is this?'

She had forgotten Henry was intolerant of all bodily ills apart from his own. He frowned, and Bella suddenly thought how much his small eyes, surrounded by ponderous folds of flesh, were like those of a pig.

'No matter. It can wait until you are restored to health, my dear. I was suggesting we crept away from all these bothersome courtiers for a few quiet days at Oatlands, but you must remain in your own apartments until you are quite well again. Then we will speak of it again. You may retire now.'

Thankfully Bella crept away, suppressing her shudders until she was safely inside the Lady Mary's suite of rooms. She sat beside the window, which overlooked the river, and wondered desperately what to do. It was serious if Henry was proposing to single her out and take her to Oatlands. Did he imagine that in the simpler environment, surrounded by just a few servants, she would prove willing to receive his love-making?

The thought made her shiver uncontrollably, and she was determined her fever or the pretence of it would be maintained for as long as possible. But would marriage to Pedro be a way out of her dilemma?

Amy looked at her in concern when she herself came to bed.

'Bella, you're so pale! Are you ill?'

'I think I must be.'

'Then get straight into bed. You can surely be excused attending the Lady Mary tonight. I'll bring you a tisane of borage and purslane. My mother always swore it was the best cure for a fever.'

'Thank you, Amy,' she murmured, and later obediently sipped the soothing drink.

But she knew her fever was not an ordinary one. It was caused by the knowledge of Charles de Nerac's perfidy, his deception in making her the object of his flattery when all he wanted was information about her mistress. Even more, she admitted much later in that sleepless night, was it caused by her own folly in liking him so much.

# CHAPTER 3

Bella was still pale the next morning when her brother sought her out. She had crept as late as she dared into the back of the chapel at Mass, hoping to avoid the King in his private pew in the gallery. Sir Thomas was waiting when she emerged.

'Come with me. I have something to say,' he growled.

Grasping her arm to ensure she didn't escape him, he led her through the Cloister Court and across the bridge over the moat. Only when they were a safe distance away from the palace buildings did he speak again.

'The King does not have endless patience,' he said curtly. 'If you continue to behave as you did last night he'll grow tired of you.'

'I wish he would!'

'You may have foolish notions, Bella,

but have you no commonsense? You could do a great deal for the family if you responded to the King's advances.'

'Would you have me the King's mistress?' she demanded hotly.

'Don't be childish! That would be a waste of effort when the King is free and looking for a wife. Of course he may wish for proof first that you are not barren, but I've no fear of that. Our family has never lacked for sons—look at my three young boys—and Jane is with child once more,' he added complacently. 'He'll marry you soon enough the moment you are known to be with child.'

'I will never be either the King's wife or his harlot!' Bella declared furiously.

Thomas sighed in exasperation. 'Do you not realise, you fool, that he needs sons? Prince Edward is four years old and sickly, and Henry cannot leave the throne to Mary. And Elizabeth's a child, still out of favour. Besides, how could a woman rule England?'

'Even if the King is capable of getting more sons, he is old. He is sick. He would most likely die before they were old enough to take his place. And remember little Prince Edward is sickly, but he's still alive.'

'Hush!' Sir Thomas glanced uneasily about, but no-one was in earshot. 'You must not speak of the King's death. It is treason!'

'It is going to happen one day.'

'Well of course, though you must never say so to anyone who wishes you ill. But, just think, Edward cannot live long. If Henry married you, and you bore him sons, and the eldest were still a child when the King died, there would have to be a Regency or Protectorate. And who better to look after the child's interests than his uncle!'

Bella stared at him in amazement. When Pedro had suggested the same thing she had dismissed it as fantasy, but it was true. Thomas did believe it was possible he might one day rule England. Was he mad, to imagine the great nobles would permit him, an insignificant country squire, to be elevated above them? She laughed.

'I can see the Norfolks and the Seymours giving way to the upstart Davenports,' she scoffed.

'Why not? They were lowly squires once. As the young King's uncle I would have the best right.'

'Better even than this imaginary child's mother?' Bella demanded. 'Tell me, Thomas, would you enjoy living when every waking minute you feared banishment to the Tower and the threat of the sword just because you once had an innocent childhood sweetheart?'

'You never had lovers like Catherine Howard was accused of!'

'Anyone wishing to gain advancement could claim I did, and how could I, any more than Queen Catherine or Queen Anne, prove otherwise?'

'It would not come to that, Bella,' he said.

'It need not be that excuse. Our aunt was a nun, now living in our home, and Henry would find that an offence easily enough if he wished. Or he might object to our Spanish mother. He has only to quarrel with the Emperor Charles again and I could be accused of treason just because of my birth!'

'Bella, you talk nonsense!' he began, but she swept on, disregarding him.

'No, Thomas, I am not going to put my head on the block for your possible advancement.'

Bella turned and stormed away towards a clump of trees. She couldn't endure to be with her brother a moment longer. It was perfectly clear Thomas had no concern for aught but himself. Even if she were forced to marry the King she would be of no more count than a brood mare, and having served her purpose would be pushed aside. If the King, that is, could do his part, and she didn't end up in the Tower after some jealous charge or convenient pretext.

If she did survive she'd never be permitted to marry again. The thought crossed her mind fleetingly, and she saw a bleak future stretching before her.

It would never come to that, she vowed. She could marry Pedro and escape to Spain. But even if that did not serve she'd rather tramp the country begging for bread, as so many of the dispossessed nuns without families to turn to had been doing since Henry had thrown them out of their convents.

She was walking across the grass so rapidly, her eyes dim with angry tears, she neither knew nor cared whether Thomas followed her. When she heard someone call her name, she picked up her skirts and ran for the shelter of the trees. She reached them and dodged behind a clump of bushes. Her foot caught in a rabbit hole and she fell heavily to the ground.

Strong arms enfolded her and she was pulled against a warm, hard body. Through the satin doublet she could feel the steady beat of a heart, and gentle fingers smoothed her hair away from her face.

'Are you hurt, Bella?'

She struggled into a sitting position as he sat down beside her, keeping one arm about her shoulders.

'You! What are you doing here?'

'I was coming to join you when you suddenly ran away from your brother,' the

Comte de Nerac said calmly. 'Have you hurt your foot?'

Cautiously Bella flexed her ankle. She hadn't done any damage, but she was breathless, and her heart was hammering so hard she thought she could hear it.

'No. Thank you. Please, let me go! We must look so foolish sitting here on the grass!'

'No-one can see us. We are hidden from view.'

'Where is Thomas?'

'When you ran off, he went towards the palace.'

'I hope he falls into the moat! Better still into the midden!'

Bella looked up at the Comte as he chuckled, and found his face much nearer to her own than she had expected. His dark eyes looked down into hers, and she caught her breath. She could almost feel the hairs of his neat beard against her cheek. She had the oddest longing to relax, to sink back against his chest and let him deal with the problems suddenly besetting her.

Then, a cold feeling spreading rapidly

through her body, she recalled he was one of those problems. He was spying on Lady Mary. He'd made himself pleasant solely in order to wheedle information from her.

She tried to struggle to her feet.

'Please let me go!'

'Am I not to have the pleasure of carrying an injured damsel back to the palace?' he asked with a laugh.

'Of course not. We would both look ridiculous. And I am not injured.'

He sighed. 'It would have been a delight to me, but I can see that an injured ankle would have deprived me of the pleasure of dancing with you, so perhaps it's as well. Besides, if you could not dance, the King would have more reason to command you entertained him with conversation.'

Bella could not control the shudder which wracked her body, and the Comte tightened his grip on her.

'My dear, what is it?'

'Let me go!' she cried, a note of panic in her voice. 'You are as bad as he! All you want is information! Thomas wants his own advancement. None of you cares about me! I wish I were back at home!'

The Comte looked at her, his eyebrows raised, but when Bella struggled to her feet he made no move to prevent her. She was able to walk back towards the palace alone, trying to calm her tumultuous emotions as she brushed off the traces of grass and leaves which clung to her skirts.

She had been intending to claim her fever had returned, but now pride came to her aid, and she dressed with especial care for supper. She chose a gown of rose-coloured damask, the bodice tight fitting with a square yoke of deeper rose, and a small ruff. The bodice dipped into a deep point, the skirt was wide, as were the sleeves, which fastened tightly at the wrists and were edged with lace. She brushed back her hair and pinned on a jaunty cap of lace, heart-shaped and set with pearls.

'Charming, as usual, Mistress Isabella. A very appropriate name,' King Henry said when he summoned her to sit beside him after supper. 'I hope your fever has gone.'

'Completely, Your Grace.'

She willed herself not to shiver as the King's small, mean eyes glimmered with anticipation and his gaze roved over her body.

The Comte was present, but to Bella's relief the King did not order him to dance with her. Instead he kept her by his side until he retired into his private Withdrawing Room.

'I have letters to deal with, my dear,' he said regretfully. 'Always the cares of state, and no-one to soothe me in moments of relaxation, but who knows how things may change? You will ride with me tomorrow morning?'

Bella could only smile and try to look gratified. It was a command, though couched as a question. Courtiers did not refuse any royal suggestion.

Once the King retired, the revels became more free. Bella saw the Comte approaching down one side of the Great Hall to where she still sat on the slight dais where the King and his favoured friends were placed. She did not want to meet him, to have to talk to him. The very thought of how closely he had held her that morning made shafts of fire course through her body.

She was too embarrassed to meet his gaze with composure, and this had puzzled her. She did not feel the same about Pedro's kisses, which were much more passionate than the chaste embrace of Charles de Nerac.

Then she recalled the Comte's true intentions, and grew hot all over as she thought of his treachery in seeking her out and uttering soft words to lull the suspicions. All he wanted was information, knowledge that could harm her mistress. He would be prepared to make love to her if it suited his purpose.

Fortunately salvation was at hand.

'Mistress Davenport, I have despaired of ever finding you alone!'

'Sir John! I thought you were in Oxfordshire?'

'I arrived earlier today. You have missed me, I dare to hope?'

She smiled brilliantly at him. Sir John Talbot was an old friend of her family, and her brother had once contemplated the possibility of a marriage. His estates were not far from their own, close to the county border with Gloucestershire, and he had acquired several new manors in the years since the monasteries had been closed. He was, as Thomas had often said before he began to imagine even higher things for his sister, a very acceptable match for the Davenports.

When he asked her to dance Bella rose quickly. She made no objection when he remained with her, and permitted him to escort her out into the garden.

'It is a warm night,' he said softly. 'Let us steal away for a few minutes.'

'I must return soon, Lady Mary will be needing me.'

'She is still talking to Eustace Chapuys. God preserve us, if she ever came to the throne that minion of the Emperor would be the real ruler of England!'

'He is just the Emperor's representative, and the Emperor is her cousin,' Bella protested as he led her from the hall and along the galleries towards the quiet, walled gardens. 'It is natural she should have much to say to him.'

'Do not let us argue about matters of state, my dear Bella. We cannot influence them.'

As they passed through the door into the gardens, a man stepped back to permit them pass. It was Pedro, and he narrowed his eyes as he recognised Bella, peering closely at her companion.

'Pedro! Do you not remember Sir John Talbot?'

'John Talbot? From Oxfordshire? But of course! I would have known if the moon was brighter. We used to get up to all sorts of pranks, you and I and Thomas. How are you, my friend?'

They talked briefly, and promised to meet again the following day to renew their acquaintance. Then Pedro said he had to go in.

'Don't steal my Bella away from me, John, if you wish for a long life!' he remarked as he left them.

'Are you and Pedro betrothed?' Sir John asked as they wandered through the garden, their eyes becoming used to the darkness.

'No, he is just my cousin,' Bella replied quickly.

'The man is clearly attracted to you. It would be a good match. I recall your mother's family was wealthy and close to the Emperor?'

'Yes, but Pedro is a younger son, and has to make his own way. He is on some mission at present, something to do with gaining the King's support for Spanish policies regarding Turkey, I believe.'

'I wanted to tell you, Bella, that I am now betrothed myself. A lady from Oxford. I hope you will wish me well.'

'Indeed I do! When do you plan to marry?'

'Quite soon, I trust. You will like Elizabeth, I am sure. She is quiet and shuns too much company, but is looking forward to living in the country and meeting my friends. If you are back at home, I hope you will meet her soon.'

Talking of his plans, they reached the end of the path and turned to walk back.

At the same moment a sound from behind them made them pause.

'Someone is crying!' Bella said softly.

'Behind that tree, I think. I can see the faint gleam of some light material. Could she be hurt?'

As they moved towards the tree, the figure which had been partly concealed by it rose, and with a muffled sob fled towards the palace.

'Poor woman! Not hurt, clearly, but in great distress. Did you recognise her?' Sir John asked.

'No, it is too dark. There's nothing we can do.'

'Most likely a lover's tiff. We had best go back. But I have been talking all about myself. How is your grandmother? Have you been home recently?'

'Not for some months. She is well, despite her great age. She was seventy last month, and she still rides round the estate putting the fear of God into everyone!'

He laughed. 'I recall her anger when Thomas and I stole some marchpane from the kitchens. I think even the King might hesitate before crossing swords with her.'

A few minutes later, after more reminiscences, she said, 'I must go in.'

As they re-entered the palace and began to climb the wide, shallow stairs, the Comte de Nerac was coming down. He bowed coldly to Bella, looked closely at Sir John, and without a word passed them.

'Who was that? I have not seen him before.'

'Oh, some Frenchman. He belongs to the embassy here to discuss Lady Mary's marriage,' Bella replied.

She could not dismiss the memory of his cold look as she helped prepare the Lady Mary for bed, and only belatedly realised that Amy was not there.

'Where is Amy?' she asked another girl.

'She said she had a fever. She was sent to bed.'

Bella knew that her own fever had been of the mind rather than the body, but all kinds of agues and fevers were commonplace in summer, by the river. As soon as she could escape from her duties, she hurried up to the room they shared.

Amy might want a drink of wine, if she were still awake.

The candle still burned, and Bella could see Amy's pink gown discarded with uncharacteristic carelessness along with her other clothes, littering the small space on the floor between their beds. Amy herself lay still, her back turned towards Bella, and did not reply when Bella whispered to her.

Bella quietly folded the gown and placed it on top of the chest, then prepared herself for bed. But she could not sleep. The Comte was angry with her. He had been so abrupt and hadn't spoken, when normally he was the most charming of men. Why? But she did not care. He was perfidious, a spy. He was nothing to her. How could he be?

# CHAPTER 4

The ride the following morning had none of the enjoyment of that stolen expedition with the Comte. For one thing Bella was deeply concerned about Amy. And the King kept Bella at his side for the first hour, everyone else remaining discreetly out of earshot.

The Comte, Bella saw from the corner of her eye, was riding with one of the young Prince's attendants, a lively, young widow whose husband had been some connection of the Seymour family. She tried not to watch them laughing and clearly enjoying one another's company. It was none of her business whom he was with, and he was a deceitful, untrustworthy man who had tried to use her to spy on her mistress. She wanted no more to do with him. Yet she could not prevent her gaze from turning in his direction.

Amy, pale and clearly unhappy, had declined to tell Bella what the trouble was. She refused to get up, saying she was too ill.

'But, Amy, can I get you anything? You must eat.'

Amy shook her head.

'Leave me alone, Bella. I am not hungry. I do not want anything.'

'Can you not tell me what is wrong? Is there nothing I can do?'

'You cannot stop men being despicable,' Amy whispered, and a wave of sobs shook her.

'Who? What has he done?' Bella demanded, but Amy shook her head and refused to say any more about what had caused her distress.

'I just want to die!' she wept. 'What else is there for me?'

Bella was anxious to return and try to comfort her friend. She couldn't miss the ride after the King's express command, but worry about Amy doing something silly made her fretful, so that she had to struggle to avoid sharp remarks which would offend the King.

Sir John Talbot and Pedro were riding as near to Bella as was comfortable with royal etiquette, and she was aware of their close regard whenever she glanced round. In a strange way it increased her uneasiness rather than comforting her.

'My dear, young lady, I must not monopolise you,' King Henry said at last with a deep sigh. He leered at her and Bella shrank inwardly. 'Tonight, at supper, I feel like being alone, apart from a few friends and gentle, pleasant company. It is a penalty of kingship that one can so rarely be away from crowds of people. Will you come and comfort an old man? And afterwards, now you are recovered from your fever, we can plan our escape to Oatlands.'

Somehow Bella made an appropriate reply, and was then permitted to drop back while the King called forward one of his gentlemen. Sir John and Pedro immediately joined her.

'You look pale,' Sir John said in concern.

'I—I feel rather ill!' she replied, wondering when she could steal a word with Pedro and beg for his help. It was becoming obvious that very soon she would have to commit herself to marriage with him in order to escape the King. There could be no more hesitation, no more maidenly qualms. Before she could say any more her brother rode up on the other side.

'Well done, Bella! He's clearly smitten! Do you not think so, Pedro?'

'He hardly ever keeps anyone with him for so long,' Pedro agreed, 'except when he's considering dalliance.'

Sir John looked at Bella with a strange expression in his eyes. 'I have heard the rumours, Bella. Are you going to be the next lady favoured?'

'You call it a favour?' she demanded hotly, and both her brother and Pedro swiftly hushed her.

'It would be a marvellous opportunity for your family,' Sir John went on.

'For Thomas, perhaps, but not for my head!' she retorted.

Sir John laughed, unconvincingly. 'Come,

my dear, he daren't get rid of any more wives! He is already a laughing stock in European courts. And he is ill. He cannot last many years. Then, you could make your own choice. Eh, Pedro?'

Bella looked at the three men in astonishment. Thomas was looking smug. Sir John seemed to be doing some difficult calculation in his head, and even Pedro, who had vowed to rescue her, was smiling warmly at her, approbation in his eyes. Hysterical laughter threatened to overwhelm her, and the men, mis-understanding, looked gratified at her shining eyes.

At length, Thomas and Sir John rode off to talk to other people, and Bella turned to Pedro.

'If I go to Oatlands the King will think I welcome his attentions. I do not!'

'You must keep him uncertain,' Pedro replied blandly. 'It will intrigue him, make him more determined to possess you.'

Bella stared at him in dismay.

'Pedro! Are you in league with Thomas? Do you wish to gain family advantage by sacrificing me? I thought you wanted to marry me. Rescue me from the King?'

'Bella, of course I want to marry you, my love! But I have been thinking more deeply about the matter. At first I could not bear the thought of you submitting to him. That was the response of the heart. Then I began to see the advantages Thomas has already discerned.'

'You mean to desert me! Betray me!'

'Bella, my dearest love, think of your duty to your family—your whole family! Do not forget that your mother was Spanish. It would be of inestimable advantage to all Europe, indeed the world, to have a half-Spanish queen influencing Henry. There is no possibility of a Spanish princess agreeing to marry him, or his winning any other European bride—'

'And with good reason!' Bella declared bitterly.

'But he needs heirs, so he has to marry another English girl. With anyone else my master would have no chance of exerting influence. Believe me, Bella, if you worked with us to secure the peace of Europe the Emperor would be grateful. And afterwards, my love, you could come to me.'

'If I hadn't died in childbed or on the block!' she flung at him as, heedless of comment, she spurred her mare into a gallop towards the trees.

She rode until she was exhausted, and then turned and found her way back to the palace. She was alternately furious and terrified. Had she really believed she was in love with Pedro? Had she been swayed merely by his kisses? Were all men so base, self-seeking and false?

It was now clear that neither Thomas nor Pedro would help her, and she dared not ask anyone else. Both had betrayed her, and she would have to depend on her own wits to escape from this intolerable situation.

She could not avoid supper with the King that evening, but she would never go with him to Oatlands and the intimacy he would expect there. As she rode, she firmly dismissed all regrets about Pedro from her mind and concentrated on making her plans.

She would ride secretly to her grand-mother's home, and beg her aid. Perhaps if she kept away from Court the King would forget her and turn to some other unfortunate. If she left soon, before he could feel too humiliated by her defection and therefore eager for revenge, she might be saved and bring no harm to old Lady Davenport. But she must go within days.

Absorbed in these reflections as she walked back from the stables, she was unaware of the Comte's approach until he spoke.

'Mistress Bella, I hope you took no harm from your fall yesterday?'

'My fall?' Bella flushed, recalling how warm and comforting it had been to have his arms about her. 'It was nothing,' she added.

'I saw you dancing last night, and hoped it put no strain on any weakness,' he went on. 'May I hope for the pleasure of dancing with you myself tonight?'

'I—' Bella paused. How could she

mention the King's command to this man? Would he understand she had no choice? Would he think she was throwing herself in the King's way, ambitious for position? Then she wondered why she cared. What was he but a spy for the French King, asking impertinent questions about Lady Mary?

'Is there to be no dancing? I understood the masque was to be in a few days, but am I mistaken?' the Comte went on, misunderstanding her silence.

'No, it is for two days hence. If you ask me, of course I will dance with you,' she added.

The Comte merely smiled, and as they crossed the moat and passed through the Great Gate he glanced up at the huge, five-storeyed gatehouse.

'This was a magnificent palace for a mere cardinal,' he murmured.

'It has been changed and extended a great deal, I believe, since Wolsey gave it to the King,' Bella replied. 'He is still making alterations to the apartments. I must go and change. Goodbye.'

She crossed the Base Court swiftly, and passed along the gallery to where she and Amy shared one of the old lodgings the cardinal had built for his guests. She was reminded of Amy's misery, and felt ashamed that, beset by her own problems, she had forgotten her friend's unhappiness.

When she reached their room, however, Amy was not there. Bella sank on to a stool and remained deep in thought for several minutes, making no attempt to change her gown.

The Comte's mention of the masque had given her an idea. If she meant to ride for home, she dared not go alone. Yet she could trust no-one to go with her. If she were attired as a boy, however, she would be safe. And many times she had borrowed some of Thomas's old clothes and ridden astride at home.

This notion had been drifting hazily at the back of her mind for some while, but until today's events she had dismissed it, believing Pedro would rescue her. Now she could no longer trust him, the idea was resurrected. Firmly she thrust away her misery at Pedro's betrayal, and concentrated on practical matters.

Until now she had made no conscious effort to plan how to acquire male clothing. The costumes for the masque, however, were stored in a small closet near the Great Hall, at the top of the stairs which led down to the kitchens.

Bella shivered with excitement. She could creep there at dawn the following day, for it was too late to set out now. Her mare was tired and there were too many people about. She could change into suitable male clothing, then make her way through the kitchens. She would be unrecognised, thought of probably as a page on some errand. From the kitchens she could reach the stables.

The prospect of escape gave her courage to endure the rest of the day. Even the King's hints that he wished for a closer relationship caused her merely to smile. When she finally retired to her room, Amy, who had been missing all day, was there, in bed but awake.

Bella looked at her closely. She was pale with red-rimmed eyes, but otherwise calm, and seemed anxious to talk.

'How was it?' Amy asked as Bella was preparing for bed. 'Did he—well, say anything?'

'He implied he dared not marry again, whatever his private inclinations, unless he was certain his wife could produce children,' Bella replied, and giggled. Suddenly, her plans for escape made, she felt carefree once more.

'So he will try them out first?' Amy gasped. 'How awful! Did he suggest—'

'Only that I might prefer to have a room closer to his own lodgings, a bigger, more comfortable room I need not share,' Bella told her.

'So he means to suggest it!'

'I suppose he could hardly ask a foreign princess to undergo such an experiment!'

'You do not seem concerned,' Amy said slowly. 'I'd be utterly terrified.'

'I am,' Bella confessed, 'but I mean to escape. First, though, what about you? What is causing you such unhappiness?'

Amy shrugged. 'A man. What else!' she said bitterly.

'Who is it?'

'It would not be fair to tell you. It is over now, and I have accepted there can never be anything. He made me think he loved me, but now he says there is no possibility of marriage, and I will not accept anything else. I mean to go home when Lady Mary will release me. Only—I do not think I can bear being about the Court and—and seeing him all the time! I wish I could leave straight away!'

Bella stared at her, plans whirling in her head.

'You live in the West, don't you?'

'Yes, near Evesham. Why?'

'I plan to leave for my home early in the morning,' she said slowly. 'It is in Oxfordshire, almost on the direct road to Evesham. Let us go together. We could both dress as men, and we'd be much safer together than alone.'

Amy, her gloom vanishing, demanded details and Bella explained.

'After we reach my home, Grandmother would send a man with you the rest of the way. It will solve both our problems.'

'But Lady Mary? We can't tell her! We can't ask permission.'

'You can send a message after you reach home and crave her pardon.'

'They will look for us when we are missed.'

'They will look for two girls,' Bella replied briskly. 'I am going in any event.'

'Then I will come, too! How shall we get the horses? Shall we ride out as if for an early ride?'

'They would want to send a groom with us. At least one of us must dress as a man first. Then they would imagine it an assignation and take little notice.'

They discussed various possibilities, and eventually decided that as Bella was taller, she would find the clothes and change into boy's attire, while Amy went openly straight to the stables. They would be more likely to escape notice separately than if they went together. Bella would bring the second set of boy's clothing and

Amy could change once they had left the palace behind.

At dawn Bella slipped out of bed. It was very early, before the sun rose, but she had been restless all night and afraid of oversleeping. She woke Amy and they silently began to dress. Bella pulled on a simple gown and flung her cloak around her shoulders, covering her head with a shawl. Giving Amy a hug and a confident smile she slipped out of the room. Amy would follow in a few minutes, as she didn't want to have to wait alone in the stables and arouse suspicion.

At the far side of the Base Court, Bella could gain entrance to the enormous range of kitchens and storerooms, close to the stairs leading to the Great Hall. She entered the low passageway past the buttery, and was for a moment unable to see in the darkness. Then she heard a footfall and hesitated, suppressing a startled exclamation.

'Bella! What are you doing in the kitchens?'

Her eyes had grown accustomed to the

gloom, and she stared in dismay at the Comte de Nerac.

'I—I came to get a posset, for Amy. She is unwell,' she stammered. 'What are you doing here?'

'It is a quick way to the stables from my lodging,' he replied.

'But—it is far too early for the King to ride.'

'I like to escape for an hour as we did that day. Would you not join me one morning?'

'I—thank you, yes, perhaps I might. But Amy—the posset—I must go.'

He stood aside courteously and Bella, chafing at the misfortune of meeting him, passed him and went into the servery. She knew he was still watching her, and had to ask one of the busy scullions for the posset. By the time he returned with it the Comte had gone, and Bella prayed he would be away from the stables before Amy reached them. She could do nothing about it, though, so she scurried up the stairs and into the closet where the costumes were stored.

She rummaged amongst the clothes and soon found a dark-blue velvet doublet which fitted her, and matching trunk hose. There was a short cloak, and a bonnet under which she was able to thrust her hair. She would have to wear her own shoes, but she had on her stoutest pair and warm stockings.

She selected another doublet of dark green, with brown trunk hose, a cloak and a bonnet.

Thrusting her old gown to the back of the heap, she rolled the clothes for Amy in her own cloak, making a bundle which she carried under her arm. Then she poked her head cautiously out into the gallery.

No-one was around. As she strolled down the stairs once more and through the series of small courtyards, she was ignored. People bustled around, carrying sides of beef and haunches of venison from the storerooms towards the great kitchens, heaving sacks of flour into the pastry rooms, and wheeling carts piled high with huge logs which were consumed voraciously by the enormous fireplaces.

At length she reached the stables. To her relief she saw the Comte riding away through the tiltyard on his black stallion. Amy was waiting in her own mare's stall, and to Bella's relief said she had been able to hide from view while the Comte waited for his horse to be saddled. The grooms were busy and took no notice of Bella as she abstracted saddles and bridles, and went to where her own mare was tethered.

Five minutes later the two girls, Bella looking dashing in her male attire, rode out of the stables.

# CHAPTER 5

A mile from the palace, Bella and Amy turned away from the river they had been following. It wound and twisted through innumerable loops, taking them far out of their way. It was easier to strike across country towards Windsor, and providing they kept the sun behind them they could not lose their way.

The going proved more difficult than Bella expected. It was low-lying ground, often marshy, and the girls had to make so many detours they ought, Bella thought more than once, to have remained with the river.

It was about twelve miles as the crow flew, half as far again by river, but it was three hours before Bella saw the ramparts of Windsor Castle looming ahead of them.

Cautiously they skirted the town on the

far side of the river, and set off on the much better road northwards. From here Bella had a better knowledge of the road. To avoid the enormous loop of the river they needed to keep well to the north, then cut through the Chiltern Hills westwards for Oxford.

An hour later, Amy having changed into her male attire and disposed of her gown in the depths of a bramble thicket, they stopped at a wayside tavern. They bought trout pasties, eating them while sitting on the bench outside.

The sun was so hot and they had slept so little during the night they both felt drowsy. First Amy leaned back against the wall of the tavern and was soon dozing. Bella decided it would be sensible to snatch a rest and leaned back herself. She pulled her bonnet down over her forehead, making sure her hair was still securely fastened and hidden, and closed her eyes.

A commotion of horses' hooves, shouts of command, and the bustle of the innkeeper coming to the door of the tavern woke Bella. She glanced up in alarm, then turned away her head in a vain attempt to hide from the new arrival.

'So there you are, without even the sense to stay hidden!'

The voice was amused, though the words were mocking. Bella looked up at the Comte and spoke with a mixture of fear and anger.

'Have you been following us? How dare you! It is bad enough you are spying on the Lady Mary, but intolerable you should follow me, too!'

Amy woke with a start.

'What is it? Who? Oh, Bella, have we been discovered?'

'Get on your horses and don't argue. They'll be here within ten minutes. We have to find somewhere secluded before we can talk.'

When Bella simply stared at him he swore under his breath, dismounted and strode across to her.

'Get the horses ready, and fast!' he shouted over his shoulder to the innkeeper, who made haste to untie the mares from the post where Bella had tethered them.

His words penetrated Bella's dazed mind and she ran to seize the saddles. As she flung on her own, the Comte dealt with Amy's. Brusquely ordering Bella to mount, he seized Amy, still bewildered and sleepy, and unceremoniously tossed her into the saddle almost before the innkeeper had fastened the girths.

'My thanks,' he called as he sprang on to his own horse.

Seeing that Bella was already urging her mare forward, he took Amy's reins into his own hands and urged both horses on. Amy, still bemused and half asleep, clutched the pommel nervously.

'What is the matter?' she gasped. 'Where are we going?'

'There is no time to talk. Hold tight!'

Soon they were galloping along the road, which wound through dense woods. A mile or so away from the tavern, the Comte slowed and turned into a narrow track curving up a steep hill.

'It is too narrow to ride together,' he said as he handed Amy's reins back to her. 'Follow me, and quietly. We are still near the road. They might hear us.'

Ten minutes later, they came into a small clearing, the ground dense with a carpet of bluebells. At one side, the trees thinned, and through a gap Bella saw a deep, narrow valley dipping away from them.

'We shall wait here,' the Comte said, dismounting.

He lifted Amy down, then crossed to where Bella still sat on her own mount. He took the reins and led the horse towards his own. When the horses were safely tied, he turned and lifted Bella down.

At his touch, she seemed to emerge from the daze which had enfolded her.

'What is it?' she demanded indignantly, only to find his hand over her mouth and his other arm clasping her tightly to him.

'Hush! Sounds carry a long way. We're being followed, by the King's men.'

Bella's heart was beating so loudly she was afraid the soldiers might hear it. She didn't know whether to believe him or not. Surely the King wouldn't send a troop of soldiers after two unimportant girls?

The Comte removed his hand, but still held her pressed against him. He turned towards Amy who had remained silent and still looked dazed.

'Talk only in whispers,' he said softly. 'We should be able to see them go past from up here,' he went on and, releasing Bella, led the way quietly to where the view of the valley and the road below was unobstructed by trees.

'They will see us out in the open!' Bella whispered urgently.

'No they will not. Lie down here,' he ordered, and before she fully understood, Bella was lying on her front, the Comte beside her, Amy beyond him, peering through a screen of fresh, green bracken.

'How did you know where we were?'

'When I came back from my own ride and joined the King, he was aggrieved because you did not appear. He sent to your lodging, but no-one knew where you were and Amy had vanished, too. Then the stable lad said your mare was gone. He had seen a strange lad riding out on it, accompanying Mistress Amy.'

'I thought they were all too busy!' Bella said, mortified.

'He saw you ride westward, and when the King sent for Sir Thomas, he confirmed you would have nowhere to go but your home in Oxfordshire.'

'But why send soldiers after us? If he did! How can I believe you?'

'You will see very soon I speak the truth. You do not know his gracious Majesty very well, my dear, do you? Despite his marked attentions.'

'Why should he bother about two girls? We are not important.'

'You are not just any girl. The King has been paying you a great deal of regard lately. Gossip was rife. To have you run away from him made him look a fool, and Henry cannot abide that. Nor can he bear to be thwarted in any way. He was very angry. He ordered a watch to be kept on all the river crossings, and sent a troop of men to Oxfordshire, to your home.'

Bella looked pale. 'Is he really furious?'

'I think one or two people hoped he

might have a seizure right there, but instead he rode off at a faster pace than I've seen him ride before. He might still fall and break his neck. I did not wait to see.'

'Thomas will never forgive me. But why did you follow us? And where are the soldiers? How did you get here before them? Is it true?'

'I slipped away immediately. I was already mounted, and a lone man can ride faster than a troop. But I will not be far ahead. When I started, my horse was already tired.'

'Why did you come?' Bella asked tremulously.

'Could I permit foolish girls to face the King's wrath alone and unprepared?'

Before she could reply, they heard the noise of several riders.

Shrinking down as far as she could in the concealing bracken, Bella peered into the valley. A troop of half a dozen soldiers came into view, their horses trotting briskly, and passed along the road to vanish behind a spur of hill.

'I am sorry I doubted you,' Bella whispered. 'Thank you for coming.'

'Do not worry. You are safe now,' he said bracingly.

'Safe? How can I be? Where can I go? They'll search for me at home. I won't be safe there!'

'You will not be there when they arrive, and no-one will know anything. They'll assume they missed you, and begin to work their way back, searching along the roads. One or two may remain, but if we can't elude them and reach your grandmother we will deserve to be caught.'

'I cannot endanger her! Not if the King is seeking vengeance!' Bella cried.

'Come to my home,' Amy suggested quietly. She was wide awake now, pale but composed, and fully understanding their peril.

'The King will send people there, too.'

'But he does not want me. They will look once and then go away.'

'We must consult Bella's grandmother. We shall not stay, but she might be able to suggest somewhere, the house of a friend who would not be suspected by either the King or your brother. I assume she would want to save you both from Henry's wrath and Bella from the dreadful fate of becoming his wife.'

Bella flushed. 'Of course she would, but I cannot permit it! Even now he might throw her into the Tower, believing she can tell him more than she knows!'

'I doubt if he would do that. It will be made clear to him that his brother monarchs may have some sympathy with a king whose queen betrayed him, but to punish an old woman just because her granddaughter has run away rather than be wooed by Great Harry would make him a mere buffoon!'

'Who would dare say that to him?'

'Ambassadors have certain privileges, and though the message may be wrapped up in layers of compliments and obsequiousness, it is fully understood! I have some influence with the French ambassador.'

'You would be in danger!'

'Would you care?'

Bella turned her head away.

'Of course I would care for the safety of anyone who had helped me,' she replied quietly. 'I am most grateful, and I will be more prudent now. What shall we do? Is it safe for us to enter taverns? How soon will it be safe for us to go home?'

'We have to remain hidden. Fortunately the nights are warm. We can sleep in the open. I can risk buying food in the villages. No-one will remark on my absence from Court, they won't be searching for me. We may need to remain hidden for a week, but we can go farther north to avoid them as they cast back.'

Bella ignored most of this.

'You are staying with us?' she demanded. 'But there is no need for that. We can manage now. We will be careful, I promise!'

'I have no intention of leaving until you are both safe somewhere. You must think ill of me if you can imagine I would.'

'I do not think ill of you,' Bella said softly. 'Thank you, monsieur.'

He looked at her consideringly until she

dropped her eyes, afraid he would read in them the confusion of her feelings towards him. He had spied on her mistress, yet he had also put himself into danger to save her.

'I think we can drop the formality as we are to be comrades,' he said briskly. 'My name is Charles. Now for plans. My horse cannot go much farther today, so we will make our way slowly northwards. We can find somewhere to sleep tonight, and tomorrow I will leave you while I go and look for food.'

The three of them rode silently through the hills, pausing to drink from a burbling stream. They avoided small villages and hamlets, though Charles ventured to buy a loaf of bread and some cheese from an isolated farmhouse, leaving the girls hidden in the woods while he did so.

Soon afterwards he said they must halt for the night.

'We still have several hours of daylight left, but our horses will be unable to carry us tomorrow if we push them too far,' he warned.

They saw to the horses, taking them to a stream in the bottom of the valley to water them, then leaving them hobbled to graze on the lush, new grass. Charles broke off pieces of the loaf, and Amy and Bella ate hungrily.

'I am so tired!' Bella confessed with a sigh when her hunger was appeased.

'Did you stay awake all night to make safe your escape?' he asked, grinning.

'Not deliberately, but I was too worried to sleep.'

'Why did you choose today?'

Bella realised he didn't know of the King's plans.

'The King bade me sup alone with him, and suggested I might like a room nearer the royal apartments,' she said briefly. 'Also he proposed taking me to Oatlands for us to be alone. I had to do something.'

'Amy, are you being persecuted by Henry, too?'

Amy shook her head.

'I want to go home, too. I'm weary of Court life,' she said briefly.

Charles, after a considering look at her, turned back to Bella.

'Your brother? Would he not help you?'

'Thomas cares for naught but becoming the next Regent of England!' she replied angrily. 'After I have done my duty, that is, and provided another Tudor prince. I don't think he's even considered the complication of dispossessing two princesses, even if the poor child Edward were to die.'

'You're safe now,' he soothed. 'We'll gather some bracken to make a bed, then you must rest.'

Thankful they had brought warm cloaks, Amy and Bella were soon fast asleep, wrapped snugly and cushioned on the soft, fragrant bracken.

For a week they rode slowly, following small tracks through the woods and avoiding habitations apart from when Charles went to buy necessary provisions.

'We must go slowly and keep well to the north, to avoid any search for you,' he insisted when Bella grew impatient.

'But they will not recognise us as boys,

98

and they won't expect you to be travelling with us.'

'If we have to share a bedroom at an inn with other travellers, your secret will soon be discovered,' he said drily. 'Besides, they know you rode off as a boy.'

She flushed in embarrassment. On the first day when he'd found her, she was concerned with her safety more than her appearance. The next morning she had been thrown into utter confusion when he'd complimented her on having excellent legs.

She'd felt naked in front of him. Until it grew too hot for comfort, she insisted on wearing her long cloak to conceal her legs.

Gradually, however, she'd forgotten. It was only when he made such a remark that she recalled her unconventional attire.

Amy, on the contrary, seemed oblivious both of her male disguise and Bella's embarrassment. She was often wrapped up in her own sombre reflections, only half attending to what went on.

'But do we have to go so far out of our

way?' Bella persisted. 'Surely the King's men will not search so far north?'

'If we keep to the south of Aylesbury Vale we stand a good chance of meeting them, or of them hearing about us. The vale itself is marshy, and there are few good roads across it. So we will be much better off in the hills to the north, even though it adds many miles to our journey. Are you so very anxious to be rid of me?' he added teasingly.

'That has nothing to do with it! I'm anxious about my grandmother. What will they do to her?'

'Nothing, once they know you have not been there. But they may linger a few days expecting you to arrive, which is another reason for delay.'

Unwillingly she accepted his reasoning, knowing it was wise, yet impatient to reach home. They travelled through the low ranges of hills connecting the Chilterns and the Cotswolds, well to the north of Oxford, and eventually made their way south again. Here there were fewer concealing woods, but Bella knew the countryside and they were able to travel by unfrequented roads.

It was late afternoon when she halted on the crest of a low hill and pointed westwards.

'My old home, though Thomas owns it now of course. His wife and children are there, so we must avoid it. Grandmother's house, which used to be her mother's, is in the next valley.'

He saw a gracious house of mellow, golden stone, built low. A church with a squat steeple was visible behind, and a village of perhaps a hundred cottages straggled alongside the banks of a small river, sprawling over a considerable area. The whole scene was bathed in the evening sunlight, peaceful and still.

To the north were barns and farm buildings, and the hills were scattered with sheep, but there were few people around. The villagers would be at supper, for harvest had not yet begun. In a month or so they would have to spend every daylight hour in the fields, gathering in the corn.

'A lovely place,' he commented lightly.

'Were you sorry to leave it when you went to Lady Mary's household?'

'It is people who make a home,' she replied quietly. 'After Thomas married Jane, and then Father died, it was not the same.'

She turned away and led them down a steep track, sunken so that they could not see above the sides. At the end was a belt of woodland, and though no path was discernible, Bella led him unerringly through until they emerged to overlook a similar valley, but much smaller and with only a couple of farmhouses visible.

'Grandmother says there used to be a village here, too, but it vanished long ago. There was a great plague and almost everyone died. The ones that were left moved into the next village.'

'We will wait until dark and then I'll go down and discover what has been happening,' Charles said.

'If the King's men are there, they will know you!' Bella protested, suddenly afraid for him.

'I will be very careful. At least there is

no inn where they might be staying.'

They concealed the horses within the wood, then sat at the edge of it, overlooking the farm and munching the mutton pies Charles had bought earlier.

'What will you do afterwards?' Bella asked suddenly. 'Will you return to Court? How will you explain your absence?'

'I will not need to. I am not accountable to King Henry, and we have been travelling between Hampton Court and Westminster, and as far as France, ever since we arrived.'

'You left when I did. They might be suspicious,' she persisted, suddenly afraid he might be in danger.

'My dear Bella, there are several hundred people in the palace, and I left after you did. No-one will connect the two.'

'So you will go back?'

Her tone was wistful, and he glanced down at her, his gaze searching.

'Would you wish to return yourself?'

Bella shuddered. 'Oh, no. How could I? I enjoyed being with Lady Mary, but I did not enjoy Court life. If she were returned to favour, and spent all her time there, even if the King forgot me, I would not wish to live so publicly. I liked it here, with just a small household, and the farm and the village. But Thomas considers that a lack of ambition. He wanted me to marry well.'

'Even he scarcely expected you to entice the King.'

She chuckled. 'No more than I did! But Thomas has the instinct to make the most of opportunities. Unfortunately he does not think far beyond the first step!'

As they talked, dusk gradually covered the landscape. Amy wandered a short distance away to sit pensively on a fallen log. Eventually, as the light faded completely, Charles rose to his feet.

'I shall go now. In case they are suspicious, and believe me to be yet another of the King's men, how may I convince them I am your friend?'

Bella thought hard, then grinned mischievously as she rose with him.

'Tell Grandmother I once hid her thimble in the secret cupboard beside the fireplace! No-one else knows that, not even Thomas or Aunt Anne. If she asks which cupboard, tell her the one the rose hides.'

'Very cryptic! I hope she remembers!'

'She will. It's where she keeps all her most precious things. I discovered it one day when I came into the room and saw her opening it, before she knew I was there. It has been a secret between us since.'

Charles had gripped her by the shoulders, and now he pulled her round to face him.

'Stay here with Amy. No creeping down after me in case you think I need help?'

She gulped. How had he known what was in her mind?

'Of course not,' she replied indignantly.

'If I catch you sneaking down after me I will make you fear me more than you do Henry Tudor!'

She gurgled with laughter. 'That's impossible! You will never be a gross, old man so fat I could never get my arms about you!'

Before she was aware of his intention

he'd drawn her close, and without conscious thought her arms slid round him, her hands meeting as she clung to him. Swiftly he bent his head towards her, and kissed her briefly.

'I trust you will never regret those words,' he whispered, and then set her aside. 'Get Amy, saddle the horses, then do not move from here, or I will not be able to find you when I come back. We may need to move swiftly if the men are still about,' he warned, and before she was aware of it he vanished silently into the deepening gloom.

# CHAPTER 6

Shaken and bewildered, Bella sank down on to the grass. That kiss had revived all the feelings she had tried so hard to repress after she realised Pedro would betray her. When Pedro had kissed her it had been exciting. She had believed he loved her and had responded by giving him her love.

Now another man's kiss reawoke in her the trembling delight she recalled from those stolen meetings in the gardens of Hampton Court Palace. But it was ridiculous. She didn't love Charles, and since Pedro had betrayed her by allowing her to see he would connive at a marriage with the King, she had fallen out of love with him, too. Hadn't she?

Bleakly, Bella found herself concluding that physical pleasure could be experienced with any attractive man, and her brother and Pedro were right that it had nothing to do with love. If that were true, how could it matter whom one married?

With grim determination, she set herself to compare her feelings towards Pedro and Charles, and came to the doleful conclusion that although there was a difference, she could not explain what it was.

The physical attraction towards a personable man was a snare, she decided. Just because a man was kind, attentive, and flattered her with compliments, it did not mean he loved her. It was naïve and gauche for her to assume that and respond by thinking she was in love with him. And it all meant nothing when she couldn't even decide what love was.

Amy seemed to know, Bella thought suddenly. Should she ask her friend to explain? Then she thought of the abject misery which had wrapped itself round Amy since they had left Court, and decided it would be unkind to try to persuade Amy to talk about a man who had hurt her so deeply.

It seemed hours to Bella before Charles returned, as secretly as he'd gone. One moment she and Amy were alone in the velvety darkness, not speaking and unable to see one another, for the moon had not yet risen. Then Charles was by her side, his hand seeking hers.

'Is everything all right? Did you see Grandmother?' she demanded, her heart racing from the fright of his sudden reappearance.

'The King's men left some days ago, although they were reported to be searching all the inns between Burford and Oxford.'

'Thank goodness!' she gasped in relief. 'Grandmother was not hurt, or frightened?'

'She wants to see you at once. Come, it's quite safe. We can take the horses down and there's a man waiting to stable them.'

She asked no more questions until they had retrieved the horses, and Bella was leading the way along the familiar path.

'How is Grandmother? Did you see her? What did she say? What had the men told her?' she asked eagerly as the track was joined by another and became wide enough for all three of them to ride together.

'Bella, my dear, she is ill. I spoke

with her for a few minutes. She wants to see you.'

'Ill? Did those devils harm her? What sort of illness?'

Bella's voice was shrill with fear, and Charles stretched out a hand to restrain her as she would have kicked her horse into a heedless, headlong gallop.

'It is nothing to do with the King, Bella. She's a very old lady, and has been ill for some weeks. She forbade anyone to tell you, as she knew you would insist on coming home. She didn't want to spoil any of your chances of advancement now Lady Mary is at Court again.'

'Spoil my chances! If only she'd known what they were! But how ill is she, Charles? Is she—'

Her voice broke and she struggled to compose herself.

'She is in very little pain, my dear. She's prepared for death, and delighted she'll have the chance to see you again before she goes. You must not distress her by showing your own sadness.'

Bella gave a shuddering sigh.

'I know. But somehow, I had expected her to be always there. She was, ever since my mother died. I cannot imagine life without her.'

'She wants to ensure your safety, then she can die happily. Try to show her that everything will be all right.'

'Of course I will!' Bella sniffed and scrubbed her eyes with the edge of her cloak.

One of the old menservants was waiting in the courtyard in front of the house and with just a few subdued words of welcome to Bella, he took the horses.

Bella, forgetting Amy and Charles, almost ran to the door, which stood open. A buxom woman of about forty waited there, and Bella threw her arms about her.

'Oh, Meg! How is she?'

'Overjoyed that she will see you once again, my lassie. Come, she is waiting, so impatient! The lady and gentleman will wait here, in the parlour.'

Old Lady Davenport was propped high on pillows. There were candles in every possible place, and Bella thought with dismay the bed looked like a bier already, ceremonial candles surrounding it.

'Bella! How good it is to see you! Come close that I may see how you look.'

She smiled and held out her hand. Bella suppressed a gasp of surprise. The hand was so thin and almost transparent. Before it had been thin, but sinewy and brown, for her grandmother had spent most of her time out of doors.

'Grandmother! Why did you not tell me you were ill?' she exclaimed as she crossed the room and kissed the old lady, then perched beside her on the high bed. 'Why did Aunt Anne not send for me?'

'I forbade her. I didn't want to drag you away from Court. But from what that young man tells me I would have been doing you a service if I had! Never mind, you are here now. And you look remarkably well in your masculine attire.'

Lady Davenport chuckled. Her voice was thin, but quite strong, and there was still a wicked glint in her eyes.

Bella blushed. 'Oh, I had forgotten! I ought to change.'

'No, now you are here I do not wish to lose a minute of your company. Tell me about this dashing Comte. Where does he come from?'

'His estates are in the Loire Valley, not far from Orleans. His parents are both dead, and he has been at the Court of Francis the First for some years. He came to England on an embassy to negotiate the Lady Mary's hand for the Duc d'Orleans.'

Lady Davenport's eyes twinkled.

'That tells me some of the practical details, but what of the man? Is he as thoughtful and kind as he appears? Do you like him?'

Bella's flushed face made it impossible for her to deny it.

'He—is very kind. I do not know why he should have taken it upon himself to help me, but without him I would have been in the Tower by now, I think!' she replied as lightly as she could.

'Hmm. And what of Thomas? Jane does not come here often, so I have little news of him.'

'He grows more ambitious by the day!

113

He wouldn't help me. He wanted me to attract the King! All he saw were the possible advantages to himself!'

'I take it you have no desire to return to Court, then?'

'No, never! Please may I stay here with you, Grandmother?'

'We must see. Now tell me all about the latest fashions. And what has the King done with Hampton Court? It is many years since I was there, and I hear there have been great building works to enlarge it, make it fit for a King.'

An hour later she sighed, looking suddenly pale and weary.

'Go and fetch the Comte, Bella. I wish to speak with him before I sleep. In the morning we will make the necessary arrangements.'

When she had relayed this message and shown Amy to the room they were to share, Bella went to find her aunt.

Anne Davenport was fifty years old, the younger sister of Bella's father. Once she had been a pretty girl, if the portrait painted when she was sixteen, which hung in the parlour, was accurate. Now she was still handsome, with a wide forehead and high cheekbones, but her body and face were gaunt and there was deep sadness in her eyes.

She smiled in genuine pleasure when Bella came into her small, bare room, and rose from the praying-stool set before a statue of the Virgin.

'Aunt? Oh, I am sorry. Do I disturb you?'

'Of course not, child. You are always welcome. Come and sit on the bed. I have nowhere else.'

The room was small and comfortless. Even now, at the height of summer, it was cold and smelled of damp. The bed was a thin, straw mattress placed on a hardboard base, with just one thin blanket and no pillow. Anne Davenport wore a heavy, woollen gown, and as Bella hugged her she felt the rough, coarse material scrape uncomfortably against the bare flesh of her hands.

Clearly her aunt, banished from her convent, sought to make her present home as much like it as she could, with its poverty and bodily mortification.

'I was with your grandmother when that Frenchman saw her. So that impossible Henry Tudor has been casting sheep's eyes at you, has he?'

'I am afraid so.' Bella sighed. 'Thomas was overjoyed, but I could not bear the thought, not even to advance the Davenports, and I am far from convinced it would have done that even if I had produced a dozen sons!'

Her aunt laughed scornfully.

'Thomas was always a dolt. If he had the slightest scrap of sense he would never have married that dreadfully opinionated woman.'

'Aunt Anne, I'm surprised at you!' Bella reproved gaily. 'Should not nuns always speak kindly of people?'

'We should also speak the truth,' her aunt said drily. 'It would have been better for the family if you had been the man.'

'Never mind me. How ill is Grandmother?'

'She will not last many more days, Bella.

116

But she has not suffered, and now her vigour has gone she will welcome death. Do not mourn for her. She would be sorry for that. She's had a full life and is ready for the next world.'

'But I shall miss her so much! She has always been here. She brought me up after my mother died.'

'We will all miss her, but that is our selfishness. She deserves to rest, to join those who went before her. Her main concern is what will happen to you.'

'And you,' Bella said slowly. 'Will Thomas permit you to remain here?'

Anne laughed in genuine amusement, and spoke with no trace of bitterness.

'Of course not. It would offend His Majesty. He cannot do anything while my mother lives, for he is afraid of her! But when she is gone, he will be more afraid of spoiling his chances with the King, and would not dare to shelter a nun in one of his houses.'

'Then what will you do? Where can you go?'

'I have plans to travel to France. It is all

arranged for me to join a convent there, and I would have gone many years since if Mother had not persuaded me to remain with her until she died. It is a more urgent problem to decide what you will do. I believe Pedro was also at Court, representing the Emperor?'

'He was in the party which came for discussions, yes.'

'There was talk some years ago of a marriage between you. You have a good dowry, and though he is a younger son he is not poor. Do you favour such a match?'

Bella was silent for some while.

'I don't think I do, not now,' she replied eventually. 'When we met, he was attentive, and I thought I loved him. He spoke of helping me to escape from the King and taking me to Spain, where Henry could neither forbid us to marry nor punish us if we did, but during the last few weeks he changed, and began to think as Thomas did. I suspect he believed a widowed queen would be a better match than a mere cousin!'

'Then we will forget him. If you had any desire for the religious life you could come with me to the convent, but I do not think that would serve. Is there any other man you might marry?'

Bella shook her head.

'There is no-one, but even if there were, no man would dare to offend the King by marrying me. He would soon find himself in the Tower. Whether the King still wanted me or not he would consider it a slight and be intent on punishment. I could not endanger anyone in such a way, either.'

'We will see. But you are safe here for a few days while we make plans. The King's men were convinced you had not been here. They won't return until they have searched elsewhere and still not found you. Now, it is late and you must go to bed. God bless you, my dear.'

That night Bella was restless, and Amy, in the other bed, tossed and turned all night, too. It was the first time for a week Bella had slept in the softness of a feather mattress, but it was also the first time for a week she had slept without the comfort of Charles's presence nearby, the feeling of security it gave her to know he would protect her from harm.

She woke early and looked across at Amy. The girl had been crying, and looked worn out with the journey and the anxiety of the past week.

Bella dressed quietly so as not to disturb her. She pulled on one of her old, cotton gowns. It was now faded and straining at the seams for she'd last worn it when she was fourteen or so, but it made her feel at home. She crept downstairs to where Meg, her old nursemaid, was already in the huge kitchen, baking bread in the long oven set in the corner of the big fireplace.

'I missed your bread,' Bella said as she tore a chunk off a new loaf and began to spread it with butter and honey.

'You mean the King's bakers cannot make bread as well as I?' Meg asked, her eyes crinkling as she laughed.

'No, nor cook pastry or roast meat as well as you do.' Bella suddenly sobered.

'Tell me the truth, Meg, how ill is Grandmother?'

'I did not think she would last so long,' she confessed. 'I believe it was those men, the King's soldiers, coming that rallied her. She knew you would be here as soon as you could, once she had heard what they had to say. She was determined to stay alive until she could help you.'

'Has she suffered?'

'No more than the usual aches. She's a great age, Bella love. It is age, nothing more. And she has had a good life. She will be happy to pass on to the next, so she would not want you to grieve for her. There are many she loves waiting for her on the other side, and one day you will meet her there yourself.'

Bella nodded. 'It is always worse for those left behind, is it not?'

'You must not fret. Tell me about this handsome young man you brought with you. French, is he not?'

Everyone wanted her to tell them about Charles, Bella thought. What could she say, apart from the fact he was handsome, kind, gracious, a good companion, a safe protector? She could not tell even Meg or her grandmother that she'd forgotten her resentment and suspicions that he was spying on the Lady Mary and come to depend on him more than anyone else. She could hardly confess she dreaded having his support removed as much as she feared being left alone when her grandmother died and her aunt went off to France.

At that moment, Meg's husband, the farm overseer, came into the kitchen. After greeting him, Bella escaped to wander over the old, familiar house she had loved as a child.

She longed to go outside, but last night both Charles and her grandmother had expressly forbidden it, saying they did not know what spies might be around, to report her presence to the King's men.

Her aunt, Meg had warned her, spent every morning at her devotions in a small room which had been furnished as a chapel. Amy was still fast asleep when Bella peeped into their room.

Charles was nowhere to be seen, but

when Meg called her to go to her grandmother, Bella found he had been closeted with the old lady for some time.

Lady Davenport looked even weaker than on the previous night. Her voice was faint, although it was clear she had lost none of her force of character.

'Bella, come in. We have been discussing where you are to go.'

'Can I not stay here?' Bella pleaded anxiously.

'It is impossible, child. As soon as I am dead the vultures will gather. You do not imagine Thomas would agree to hide you, do you?'

Bella shook her head. 'No, nor Jane. So where must I go?'

'It would be dangerous for them, even if they were willing. And you could not hope to remain hidden until the King died. That is what it would mean, Bella,' Charles said gently. 'It is too dangerous for you to stay in England.'

She looked from him to her grand-mother, who was nodding her head.

'I do not want to leave you,' she said quietly.

'You must. I shall last very little longer. I want to have your promise so that I may die peacefully.'

'Where must I go? Have you friends I could go to, perhaps?'

'You might go to your mother's people in Spain.'

'But I know nothing about them! I can write a little Spanish, and have written a few letters to them, but I don't speak Spanish and they would not want me.'

'It would be hard for you, my child, I know. In Spain they keep women secluded, far more than here. After the freedom you have enjoyed, it would be difficult to conform. But there is little alternative.'

Bella wondered suddenly whether they would constrain her to marry Pedro. Would he want her still? Or would he be angry that she had spoiled her chance to become Queen of England? She had never been really sure whether she wanted to marry her cousin, or whether she had been misled by the physical excitement his kisses awoke in her. After his willingness to see her wed to Henry Tudor she knew she could never marry him.

'I think I would prefer almost anything else,' Bella said, trying to smile cheerfully.

'That is what I thought. Charles, would you leave us for a while? Bella will come to you later.'

'Of course.'

He bent to kiss Lady Davenport's hand, and they smiled like old friends. Bella wondered briefly, for her grandmother did not normally choose to address virtual strangers by their given names on such short acquaintance. But she had little time left, Bella recalled with a pang. There was no more leisure for her to cultivate friendships.

Charles left the room, quietly closing the latch, and Bella spoke slowly, working out a new plan as she did so.

'I do not wish to become a nun,' she said slowly, 'but perhaps I could travel to France with Aunt Anne, and live at her convent until Lady Mary marries the Duc d'Orleans. Then I might beg her to take me back into her service. Only I have no money, and Thomas would certainly not make me an allowance.'

'That need not concern you. It would solve the problem of where you are to find a home, although I do not like the idea. Go and look in the cupboard, and bring the leather pouch to me.'

Puzzled, Bella went to the wall which was covered, like some of the rooms in Hampton Court Palace, in graceful linenfold panels. She found a particular rose carved in the surrounding frieze, and twisted. One of the panels slid back, revealing a shallow cupboard in which there was an old, wooden box and a large, leather pouch.

She removed the pouch, closed the panel and took the pouch over to the bed.

On her grandmother's instructions Bella opened the pouch and poured out on to the bed a collection of jewels that made her gasp in amazement.

'Grandmother, where did all these come from?'

'Your grandfather loved giving them to

126

me. But I want you to take them. I cannot leave you anything else. Thomas would find it difficult to send money to you, even if he were willing, and you cannot have this house as I had planned. If you leave England he might refuse to give you your dowry. These jewels are worth far more than the dowry settled on you, and would be enough to keep you in comfort for the rest of your life, if necessary.'

Bella was still speechless, and Lady Davenport plunged her hands into the pouch, giving a grunt of satisfaction as she discovered what she sought.

'Here,' she said in triumph, holding up a long, wide, leather belt. 'I had this made for travelling. You can wear it under your gown.'

'Thank you, oh, thank you!' Bella whispered.

'Good. Now put them back into the pouch and take them to your room. You can fill the pockets later, and be ready to leave the moment I die. Can I have your promise? I have already made your aunt promise me the same, so you can travel together. The moment I go, news will get to Jane, I have no doubt, and she will be over here within the hour. You must be gone before then.'

'I promise,' Bella said reluctantly.

Five minutes later the indomitable Lady Davenport was explaining to Charles she wished him to escort Bella and her aunt to France, to a convent near Bordeaux.

'It is not what I wished for her,' she said with a sigh. 'But there is no alternative as she has enraged the King.'

'There is one alternative,' he said softly, turning to look at Bella who sat on the other side of the great bed. 'Bella could marry me.'

# CHAPTER 7

Lady Davenport's sigh of relief was intense and audible. Bella, who had been staring in amazement at Charles, turned to look at her grandmother.

'My dear boy! Now I know she will be safe! I can die at peace.'

'But—' Bella started to protest, her voice faint with surprise, but Charles spoke at the same time.

'I will make arrangements as soon as possible. Is there a priest here you can trust? Someone who will not betray us to your son or the King's men?'

Lady Davenport shook her head.

'Unfortunately not. The local man's a reed, swaying with every breeze. Once I am gone he would feel no loyalty to me or Bella. You must marry in London, or France if there is no time to wait. I know I can trust you.'

'You look tired. We'll leave you to sleep, since we have much to discuss.'

He bustled Bella out of the room, his look warning her against speaking.

'Yes, I know you were going to say something foolish,' he told her when they were coming down the stairs. 'Just think. Your grandmother is dying. She's concerned for your safety. This has made her happy.'

'I do not want any man to marry me out of some ridiculous sense of duty, to make a dying woman happy!' Bella flared at him.

'Who said that was my reason?' Charles asked mildly. 'Why should I wish to make a woman I have only just met happy by sacrificing my entire life to a marriage I did not want?'

'So it was all a pretext? You did not mean it? You just said it to ease her mind?' Bella didn't know whether to be angry at his deception or relieved she wouldn't be hustled into marriage with a man who didn't want her.

Her grandmother's suggestion had taken

her utterly by surprise. She had never for a moment considered marriage with Charles de Nerac, but for one blindingly revealing second she had seen it as the answer to all her prayers.

She had not stopped to consider whether she loved him or not. She just knew that the idea of spending the rest of her life in his company, safe and secure, cherished and cared for, free of the complexities of life and the dangers which surrounded her, was a promise of bliss. And then she'd recalled the few occasions when he held her close, and most of all that brief kiss the previous night, and a glow of excitement had consumed her.

It was cut short by the recognition of reality.

In other circumstances, if he'd loved her, she would gladly have married Charles de Nerac, but she would take no man who thought it a duty.

'Thank goodness there is no-one here to do it then!' she commented tartly. 'Once Grandmother is dead, you need pretend no more! I certainly would not want you to carry out a promise you felt had been forced on you! And I would expect to be consulted about my own marriage, especially now I do not have to obey my brother's wishes!'

She eluded his hand as he reached out for her, and forgetting the ban on leaving the house, ran towards a door opening into the stable yard. Once there she crossed to the stables and scrambled up the ladder into the hayloft. He still had not appeared as she dragged the short ladder up after her and she began to feel rather foolish. No doubt he would not have pursued her, she was being so dramatic.

She flung herself down on a pile of new, June hay. If only it had been different! If only Charles loved her! How willingly she would have married him.

It was, however, impossible. Her grandmother should not have extracted that promise. Even if she'd not put the suggestion to him directly, she must have hinted strongly enough to make Charles feel obliged to offer.

At least they understood it was all a

pretence. Once Lady Davenport died, he could go his way. How unfortunate it would have been if, through helping her escape the King, he'd been forced into an unwelcoming marriage.

A short while later she heard Meg shouting her name.

'What is it, Meg?' she called.

'Your friend is awake. Will you come and find her some old gowns of yours?'

Ashamed to have forgotten Amy, Bella quickly scrambled down from her hiding place and went back into the house.

'Did you sleep well?' she asked Amy while she sought in the chest for another gown.

Amy sighed. 'I think I must be used to sleeping in the open. I did not sleep till almost dawn. I am ashamed to have slept so late! How is Lady Davenport? I ought to have been paying her my respects if she is well enough to see me.'

'She has been busy enough, despite her illness!'

The bitter note in Bella's voice caught Amy's attention.

'What is it?' she asked. 'Is she angry with you for running away?'

Bella shook her head, and swiftly related what had occurred while Amy slept.

'So you see, I cannot possibly marry him! Not when he is constrained by politeness and concern for my grandmother to suggest it,' she finished dolefully.

'Do you love him?'

Miserably, Bella nodded. 'I did not know, till Grandmother suggested it. I have been an utter fool, Amy! I liked him, felt comfortable with him, was restless when he was away from me, but thought nothing of it. I expected something different, like it was when Pedro kissed me, though even that was not right, I was so confused. But I will not marry him when he does not want it.'

'Do you not think you should accept the offer and hope he comes to love you, too?' Amy asked slowly.

'No! I could not. It would be cheating him!'

'Most marriages are based on much less, few start off with love,' Amy said. 'He does

134

not love anyone else, so why should he not come to love you?'

'I do not know, but I could never be happy if I felt he had been forced to marry me.'

'Then you are a fool, Bella! Do you remember I once told you that when you were in love you would not need to ask me if it was real?'

'Yes,' Bella replied, 'but what difference does that make?'

'I already knew what it meant to love hopelessly, knowing my love could never be returned,' Amy said fiercely. 'If I had the slightest opportunity to marry him, whether he loved me or not, I would take it eagerly! I would have the happiness of being with him, make sure he came to love me in the end. It would give me a reason for living which I do not have now!'

Bella stared at her friend, aghast at her vehemence.

'Amy, I am sorry! I did not realise it hurt so much! But I am not like you. I could not do it.'

'I hope you are not sorry when you

come to realise what you have lost,' Amy replied.

Later that afternoon, when the two girls were sitting in the parlour while Charles and Anne were with Lady Davenport, Amy revived the subject.

'Bella, if you are truly determined not to marry Charles, come and stay with me in Evesham. You need not bury yourself in the convent with your aunt.'

'But—it would be dangerous for you all,' Bella said slowly.

'If you do not want to, please say so,' Amy said rather stiffly.

'It is not that at all! I would love to stay with you, but surely once the King hears you are home, he will send men to punish us.'

'I have been thinking about that,' Amy said slowly. 'He has no reason to bear me malice. I can say I had a sudden summons home, illness. Once my parents have heard about it they will support me.'

'But I would bring danger to you all,' Bella pointed out. 'The King will want to punish me for slighting him.'

'No-one in Evesham knows you, and it is far enough away to be safe from an accidental meeting with anyone who does. We can say you are my cousin come to visit. Mother has an enormous family living all over England, for both her parents had a dozen brothers and sisters, and most of them had many children, too. I do not even know many of my real cousins, and no-one else can possibly remember all of them. I am sure it would be possible, and safe.'

'I could not live the rest of my life with your family, though.'

'You have the jewels, sufficient dowry for anyone who wanted to marry you. I am sure you would not have to remain with us for long,' Amy said bracingly.

'I could not marry anyone but Charles.'

'You may think that now, but maybe you will forget him. I do not intend to languish just because I cannot marry—the man I want to. I shall take the first pleasant man who offers, and make what I can of my life.'

Bella smiled bleakly. She could not

imagine it, but Amy's invitation was a way out, and she would deal with any problems later on.

'When should we tell Charles that I am not going to London with him?'

Amy had it all worked out.

'He told me he intended to escort me to my home before taking you to London. We spoke of it while you were with your grandmother after dinner, and apart from feeling responsible for me, he said it would be better to travel to London by way of Buckingham and St Albans, north of the route we took coming here. If we waited until I have spoken to my mother, then tell him you are staying with me, there will be nothing he can do. He cannot abduct you from our house.'

Bella was far from satisfied. She was not at all sure that the Comte de Nerac wouldn't find some way of constraining her if he wished, but she could hope he would be so thankful to be relieved of his promise, that he would accept her decision. It wasn't, she thought mournfully, as though he wanted her himself.

For two more days, Lady Davenport lingered, growing weaker, but clearly content that she had provided for Bella's future. Bella felt twinges of guilt when she sat with the old lady and smilingly nodded at all her comments of how happy she would be with the Comte de Nerac, but consoled herself that she was making her grandmother's last days more peaceful and content.

It was early the following morning when Meg called out to Bella.

'Your grandmother, she's worse. Come quickly, Miss Bella!'

Bella raced towards her grandmother's room.

Lady Davenport lay on the bed, her face as white as the sheet, her blue eyes the only colour in her. Charles sat at the far side of the bed, holding one paper-thin hand in his large brown ones. Aunt Anne kneeled beside her mother, her head bowed, and Lady Davenport's hand rested on her daughter's grey hair, for once not concealed by the nun-like coif she usually wore.

As Bella entered the room, the old lady's glance turned to her, and a smile lit up her face. All the lines of a long, sometimes hard life had been smoothed away, and she looked oddly like the young girl she'd once been.

'My dearest child, so like your mother! She made my boy so happy!' Lady Davenport said breathlessly.

Bella approached and kissed her.

'Do not try to talk, Grandmother,' she said gently.

'No. There is no more to be done.'

'Shall I call the priest?' Bella asked.

'He was here yesterday. He did all he could. He cannot do more, and if he came you would have to go. I would rather spend my last hours with my loved ones, child.'

Twenty minutes later it was all over. Lady Davenport had lain there, looking at Bella, peace in her eyes. Then she'd whispered a faint, 'God bless you, child,' and closed her eyes. Imperceptibly she ceased breathing, and it was only when her head fell sideways that Bella realised the end had come.

Charles came round the bed and gently prised her fingers loose from where she convulsively clutched the bedcovers, then he lifted her bodily and carried her from the room.

Once in her own, small room Bella gave way to tears, and Charles sat and rocked her until the first storm of grief abated.

'My dear, we must leave,' he said gently. 'We must do as she wished. She was happy to go, once she'd seen you.'

Bella sniffed and nodded.

'The horses are all ready, saddlebags packed. When your aunt is ready we will be away.'

They went downstairs and found a tearful Meg in the kitchen busy packing bread and cheese and meat pies into parcels inside clean napkins.

'You can keep away from towns for several days with this to feed you,' she said quietly. 'God bless you all, and if you can ever come back safely, afterwards, Miss

Bella, come and see us again.'

Amy was already out in the stables, and a few minutes later a composed Aunt Anne came out to join them.

'We will talk when we are safely away,' she said quietly as Charles lifted her on to the quiet horse she normally rode when she had to make journeys.

Within an hour of Lady Davenport's death, they were gone, out of the valley she had loved, away from Bella's home.

They rode silently, Anne leading. Bella scarcely cared where she went, she was so numb with misery, and did not for some time realise that they were riding westwards, on the road to Gloucester, instead of turning northwards at Burford towards Stow-on-the-Wold and Evesham.

'Where are we going?' she asked suddenly.

'I will explain when we stop to eat,' her aunt replied.

They stopped beside a clump of tress to eat some of the bread and cheese, and Bella found that she was unexpectedly hungry.

'I am not coming to London with you,' Aunt Anne said quietly after she had carefully refolded the napkins and stowed them in the saddlebags.

'Not coming? But why? Are you not going to France?' Bella demanded.

'Oh, yes, but it was all arranged long ago, before you and Charles came,' Anne replied. 'The two of you will travel faster than I can, and my bones are stiff. I cannot contemplate such a long ride across the width of both England and France when I can travel more comfortably and directly. There is a friend in Northleach, the brother of one of my former sister nuns, and he will escort me to Gloucester where I can be taken by boat to Bristol, there to join a ship calling at Bordeaux.'

'Will you be safe on your own?' Bella asked, fear for her aunt overcoming her own sudden sense of loss at the imminent parting.

'Of course. The people involved are all trustworthy, and I will be escorted the whole of the way. I would suggest you came with me, Bella, but I am afraid they would not take Charles, too, and Bordeaux is a long way from Orleans. You could not travel through France on your own to rejoin him.'

'If that is what you wish, Aunt,' Bella said slowly. 'It is sudden, losing you, too, but I can see the journey by boat will be much easier for you.'

Charles questioned Aunt Anne closely, but seemed satisfied by her replies, and when they rode into the small village of Northleach and met the miller there, who had made the arrangements on Anne's behalf, he declared himself content.

'I shall remain here for one night, and be in Gloucester tomorrow,' Anne said. 'God bless you, Bella. Send word to me once you are safe in France.'

Bella nodded, and clung to her aunt.

'Take care!' she whispered. 'I pray you will arrive safely.'

Her aunt smiled serenely.

'I have trust in God. Do not grieve, child. My mother is in a better place, and I shall be resuming my vocation.'

Bella nodded. Already, behind the

144

natural grief at the loss of her mother, her aunt looked more peaceful, and Bella sensed she was eager to return to her religious life with as little delay as possible. The journey from Bristol would be far quicker than overland by way of London.

'I am content to know you have a good man to care for you, and that we shall be in the same country, both of us safe from that deplorable monster on England's throne.'

Torn between laughter at her aunt's irreverent contempt for her secular King, and sadness at leaving her, for a moment Bella could not speak. Then she managed to bid her aunt farewell, and permitted Charles to lift her back on her own horse.

It had been late morning when they had started, and by dusk they reached the steep escarpment which swept down towards the Vale of Evesham.

'We will stay here for the night,' Charles decided. 'Do you mind not going to an inn? I would prefer to keep out of sight in case Henry still has his spies looking for us.'

'There is a wood halfway down,' Amy said. 'Look, to your right. We would be sheltered there.'

While Charles and Amy made the usual bed of bracken, Bella sat to one side, still unaware of them in her grief.

Obediently she drank from the skin of wine Meg had provided, and bit into one of the pies. After one mouthful she wrapped it up again in the linen napkin. Then she rolled herself into her cloak and, still wordless, curled up to sleep. She was quite oblivious when Charles lay quietly beside her and when he saw she was shivering, put his own cloak over her for extra warmth.

'Hush, my love. She did not suffer,' Charles said when, in the middle of the night, Bella awoke and began to weep, deep, silent sobs.

Bella wasn't aware of his arms about her, his body warm and strong, close to hers, but she was comforted. She slept again, and it was only as the first streaks of dawn lit the sky that Charles gently drew away from her.

They woke early the following morning and finished their bread and cheese. Soon they could be eating more in Amy's home.

This was a small, manor house some miles north of Evesham. Still wary of possible spies, Charles forded the river to the east of the town, and by mid-morning they were riding along the lane which approached the house.

The fields were busy with men, women and children gathering in the hay, and in a nearby orchard, the birds vied with the cherry-pickers for the lush red fruit. But in the stableyard of the manor house, the expected bustle was muted, only one young lad desultory sweeping out an empty stable.

'What is the matter? Where is everyone?' Amy cried out in sudden alarm, and, without waiting for help, dismounted from her horse and ran towards an open door at the back of the house.

'Can the King have taken them?' Bella asked swiftly.

'It is unlikely, or there would be men here,' Charles said reassuringly, but he looked anxious and leaped down from his horse.

Bella found herself dropping into his arms as she slid from her own horse at the same moment he came to lift her down. They heard raised voices from the house, and turned, still embraced, to see Amy emerge, followed by a huge, villainous-looking man brandishing a knife almost as large as a sword.

'Amy!' Bella shrieked.

The man dropped his knife and stood, a vacuous smile on his face as he wiped greasy hands down the front of the already dirty smock he wore.

'They be in Lunnon Town,' he said, nodding his head vigorously. 'Took off a week since, they be.'

# CHAPTER 8

'London? The Tower?' Bella demanded. 'Did the King's men take them prisoner?'

Amy shook her head.

'No. It's nothing whatever to do with the King. His men have been here and Will—this is Will, he's our cook—says there are still strangers at the inn.'

'Your parents, why are they in London?' Charles asked calmly.

'My sister has been brought to bed with twins, and Mother was so delighted, for they are her first grandchildren, nothing would do for her but to go to London to see Kate.'

'Thank goodness for that.' Bella sighed. 'For a moment I believed the worst.'

'It is difficult. I do not know what to do. It could be dangerous for us both to remain here without any protection, until they return.'

'You certainly may not stay here alone. You must come to London with us, Amy,' Charles said. 'We can escort you to your parents there.'

Bella suppressed a sigh. She knew they dared not remain at Amy's home alone, since it appeared the King's men were still hunting for them. But she did not relish journeying farther in Charles's company. It would be too painful.

Amy and Charles sat on stools by the kitchen table, talking as they spooned up a surprisingly tasty rabbit stew which Will had ladled out on to huge, wooden platters. Bella was deep in her own thoughts.

Taking refuge with Amy's family had appeared the only course open to her, but now they all had to go to London she began to consider other possibilities. Would it be safe for her to stay in London? Surely in such an enormous city she could remain hidden from Henry's vengeful eyes. Yet what could she do there?

She could not live alone. It would hardly be fitting, and she did not wish for it. To adopt the guise of some lowly job, becoming a tavern wench or maidservant to some city magnate, had no attraction. She was too young to hope for a position managing a household for an elderly widower. Yet what else was there?

Amy had suggested she might, with her dowry of jewels, soon find a husband. If that had been possible in the sparsely-populated countryside surely it would be even more practicable in the bustling city? She would still need help, however, someone with whom she could live.

Bleakly she accepted this was the only possible future for her. She dared not return to Court; she had rejected her brother and his family, and after Pedro's betrayal could not claim refuge with her Spanish cousins. She could not live alone, and she would never marry the man she loved but who did not love her, so she might as well make the best of a loveless marriage.

Thinking that her silence was due to unhappiness at the death of her grandmother, Charles and Amy did not try to include her in their planning. Bella was content to leave it to them, and listlessly nodded when Charles decreed they must set off immediately.

'We cannot remain here even for one night,' he said after listening to Will's account of the strangers staying in the village. 'As soon as Will has packed us some food we must be off.'

They rode southwards for a while, as though heading for Gloucester, but when they were safe in the concealment of a thick belt of woodland they turned east and set off along less frequented ways. On the second day, they passed through Banbury, and with no sign of pursuit they relaxed.

Over the next few days Bella recovered her poise. She had plans, of a sort, for her future. The pain of one loss became more bearable, and she firmly suppressed her longing for Charles. She concentrated on the memory of her grandmother's pleasure in seeing her again, and knew she had helped the old lady die peacefully with someone she loved beside her.

She followed silently as Charles directed

them to London. For greater safety she and Amy retained their masculine clothes, but as they paused for the last night a few miles north of the city, Amy suggested they changed into gowns.

'My mother would think it a great jest, but my father is more sober. He might be offended.'

'It is safe enough now,' Charles agreed, and on the following morning the girls were once more decorously garbed as they rode the last few miles towards London, wearing their cloaks to shield them from a sudden heavy shower.

'At least you will not be installed here as one of Henry's women,' Amy said cheerfully as they approached the village of Islington.

Bella looked at the large, prosperous houses lining the road and frowned.

'Here?' she queried. 'Surely these are houses belonging to rich merchants?'

Amy pointed to the east.

'The King has hunting lodges hereabouts, and it is reputed he uses one at Newington Green to house his mistresses,' she explained.

Bella shuddered. 'I do not want to be reminded of it,' she exclaimed.

'Shall we stop to eat? It is past noon,' Charles asked, and when the girls agreed he turned aside towards a tavern nestling at the edge of the green.

There were several people sitting outside, enjoying the now warm summer sun and watching the carts and horsemen trundle by on the road, one of the main routes to the North. Charles dismounted and turned to lift Bella down. Then he went to help Amy as an ostler came to take the horses, and Bella looked about her with reviving interest. She stepped aside hurriedly to avoid a cart laden high with barrels, almost collided with another man who was carrying a large basket on his head, and then her foot slipped on the wet, greasy cobbles.

She stumbled, just as two men on horseback approached in a flurry of haste, and for a moment thought she would fall under the flailing hooves.

Before she could recover her balance, hands reached out and caught her round the waist. Unable to draw breath to cry out she found herself hoisted across the neck of one of the horses, and as she sprawled, kicking furiously to free herself, a hand was clamped roughly across her mouth.

'It is too late, dear sister. We have you safe!'

'And before you are released, pretty cousin, you'll be mine!'

As Bella was carried away, Amy, still on her horse, screamed and pointed.

'Charles, they have Bella! Oh, quickly!'

She wrenched the reins from the hands of the startled ostler and kicked her horse into motion. With an oath, Charles threw himself on to his horse again and set off after her. Soon they were galloping side by side along a narrower road to the east of the main one, lower down but still heading northwards.

'It was Thomas, her brother,' Amy gasped.

'Who else? There are just the two of them, I think,' Charles said grimly, as he followed the fleeing figures a short distance ahead.

'I—think it was Pedro,' Amy said slowly. 'Have they been following us all this time?'

'Save your breath for riding,' Charles advised. 'And when we catch up with them keep well out of the way! I cannot follow two abducted girls!'

He said no more, but concentrated on gaining ground. The houses had thinned now, and they were surrounded by lush fields and orchards. It was open country and he had no fear that his quarry might escape him in amongst thick trees. That was one advantage, another that the doubly-laden horse was unable to travel fast.

Thomas and Pedro, however, had fresh mounts. His own had been ridden hard for several days, and was weary. He had to catch them quickly before the beast foundered.

As he rode, he was struggling to undo the fastenings holding the saddlebags in place, and with a grunt of satisfaction felt them loosen. He cast them aside and perceptibly his horse's stride lengthened.

He was slowly overtaking Bella and her captors.

Bella, too, was helping, he noted with satisfaction. With no time to secure her properly, or even to haul her into a more convenient position in front of him, Thomas was having difficulty managing the horse.

His burden was both unusually heavy and unbalanced. The creature was not responding even to the vicious spurs Thomas used unmercifully. Uncomfortable, confused by the commands to stop which Bella was shouting almost in his ear, and her tugs on his mane, the horse suddenly reared.

Thomas, struggling to remain in the saddle, let go his hold on Bella, who completed the horse's demoralisation by using both feet and hands to push herself away from him. As she fell to the ground in a tangle of petticoats, the horse bolted.

Thomas, half unseated and clinging in an undignified manner to the pommel, was swept past Pedro as the latter turned to find Charles beside him.

'Bella! Are you hurt?' Amy, some way behind Charles, flung herself out of the saddle and ran to her friend. Bella was sitting up, rubbing her elbow.

'I shall have a few bruises,' she said ruefully. 'Thank goodness that storm softened the ground. Charles!' she added in alarm, as she sat up and saw the two remaining men circling a few feet away, swords drawn.

She struggled to her feet and would have rushed towards them, but saw in time that this might distract Charles. Drawing back with Amy into the shelter of a large oak tree, they stood and watched.

Charles had the advantage of knowing his horse, a beast he had ridden for many weeks, and despite the unusual manoeuvrings being asked of him, the animal was responding obediently.

Pedro's mount was clearly a hired hack, and just as clearly afraid and resentful of the whistling swords singing past his head. He danced away, giving neither man an opportunity of closing with his opponent. Charles pressed closer, and then suddenly, with a slashing cut, severed one of the reins close to the bridle.

Now Pedro's horse was totally out of control, and the sudden tug on the rein unnerved him completely. He whirled aside, and set off after his companion, leaving Pedro struggling to his feet a few yards away from Charles.

To Bella's dismay she saw Charles discarding the advantage of being mounted, and leaping to the ground. The fool! She clenched her fists and wondered wildly why men had to pay such attention to notions of honour. If she'd had such an advantage over an enemy she'd never have given it up.

Pedro, grasping his sword firmly, and with a short but lethal-looking dagger in his left hand, advanced. As Charles awaited him, unmoving, a look of confidence spread across Pedro's face.

'The girl is nothing to you. Why do you not leave her with her family?' he taunted.

Charles disdained to reply, apart from lowering the point of his rapier so that it was directed at Pedro's heart.

Unable to provoke Charles into a verbal response, Pedro suddenly sidestepped and then lunged forward. Charles was ready for him and with his own dagger parried the stroke, while lunging forward in his turn.

They were evenly matched, though Pedro favoured the older methods of slashing cuts while Charles adopted a quieter, though notably effective technique of short, swift movements which were so fast his opponent often only saw them belatedly.

Amy, her gaze fixed unwaveringly on the combatants, moved gradually closer, unaware of what she was doing. No-one noticed the huge, black cloud which was rapidly approaching until a sudden roll of thunder made Charles's horse snort in fright.

Startled, Bella looked round. With an irrational surge of triumph and confidence that Charles would be the victor, she suddenly realised that if Charles's horse took fright at the thunder and bolted they would be stranded with one horse amongst them. She moved slowly towards it, and grasped the bridle.

Standing beside the trembling horse, stroking his nose and murmuring gently to calm him, Bella sensed that Pedro was tiring. His lunges became wilder, and once he missed his footing and but for an agile recovery would have been at Charles's mercy.

Charles intensified his attack, his own sword strokes coming with increasing rapidity, and suddenly an unexpected twist of his blade when Pedro parried it with his dagger sent the dagger flying out of Pedro's hand.

Now Pedro was at a disadvantage, but, leaping backwards out of harm's way, he dragged a second short, slender dagger from a sheath at his belt. It was too fragile to use for parrying the heavy sword, but this was not Pedro's intention. Moving backwards to gain space and time, he suddenly flung the small dagger directly at Charles.

Bella bit back a gasp of dismay, but to her relief Charles anticipated the move. He ducked sideways and then flung himself on Pedro, a fierce assault that bore the other man backwards for several paces.

Then Pedro simply stopped fighting. As he dropped his sword to the ground and stood looking past Charles, Bella realised something odd was happening. Before she could move, Pedro, ignoring Charles's threatening blade, leaped forward and Charles just had time to swing his weapon sideways to avoid impaling Pedro on it.

'Amy!'

Bella swung round. She had forgotten her friend, hidden from her by the horse she was holding. Now she saw Pedro kneeling on the ground, Amy in his arms, and blood pouring down from a wound in her arm where the dagger had stabbed her.

'Quick, something to staunch the blood!' Pedro ordered, and Bella frantically fumbled with her petticoat to tear off a strip.

'She has swooned. It is no more serious,' Charles said calmly, as he went to Amy's head and supported her while Pedro tied the bandage in place.

'My God, Amy, I might have killed you! I did not see you there! What are you doing here? Just a short distance to the side and I would have killed you! Amy, forgive me!' Pedro muttered frantically to himself.

'We passed a small inn a short way back. Let us get her there,' Charles suggested practically.

Pedro glanced up at him, gradual recollection of the fight returning. He nodded, but did not speak.

'My horse is the stronger beast. Hand her up to me,' Charles directed as Bella went to retrieve the two remaining horses.

Pedro seemed to come back to life.

'No! I must carry her. Is that her horse?' he demanded of Bella.

'It is not big enough to carry a double load,' Charles objected.

'It will have to! It is not far, and I am not permitting anyone else to carry her! Besides, you'll have to take Bella,' he added.

'As you wish. We must get her indoors

as soon as possible, as there's another storm brewing,' Charles pointed out. Without a further word, Pedro mounted Amy's horse and when Charles lifted her up cradled the unconscious girl tenderly against his breast.

'A cloak,' he demanded imperiously. Charles silently unstrapped the cloak Amy had been carrying behind the saddle and handed it to Pedro. He draped it carefully to protect Amy from the heavy spots of rain which had begun to fall, and without a word, set off back the way they had come.

Charles lifted Bella on to his own horse and climbed into the saddle.

'Intriguing,' he murmured as he moved off after the others. 'What do you suppose all that meant?'

'Amy told me she loved someone who couldn't, or wouldn't, marry her,' Bella said slowly. 'She would never reveal who it was, and I had no idea from her behaviour. If it was Pedro, it explains why she could not confide in me.'

'Because before he decided it would

be advantageous to match you with the King he wanted you himself?' Charles surmised. 'I very much fear, my love, that his affections tend towards Amy! Are you mortified?'

'I am sure I never loved him anyway,' Bella said carelessly. 'It must have been Amy that night, in the garden,' she went on thoughtfully.

'What night?'

'It was the same day you saw me in the park, when I fell,' she said slowly, sorting out her recollections. 'That evening I met an old friend, Sir John Talbot.'

'I saw you with him later,' Charles remarked.

'As we went out into the garden, we met Pedro coming in,' Bella went on, 'and in the garden we saw a girl crying. She ran away when we approached, but she was wearing a pale dress. When I got back to my room Amy had thrown a pale pink gown on the floor, and was in bed. The following day she was ill, and made some bitter remarks about men.'

'And was content to leave the Court

when you decided to run away.'

'Poor Amy! How can men be so despicable!'

'I rather think your cousin has realised where his true happiness lies,' Charles said drily. 'Shall we help promote a match? Do you wish to have your friend married to someone willing to intrigue against you?'

'If she loves him, why not? Besides,' she added mischievously, 'if he is safely wed Thomas cannot constrain me to marry him now the King has apparently lost interest in me.'

'Has the King said so?'

'According to Thomas. In between cursing me and his horse, during that most uncomfortable ride, he said if I agreed to marry Pedro and make it appear that I ran away to him, he could placate King Henry and the Davenports would be back into favour. Not such high favour, naturally, but not banished from Court. Oh, look, aren't those your saddlebags?' she added, pointing.

Charles retrieved them from the ditch where they had been discarded, and there was no time for more speech. They soon reached the tiny, thatched inn, and Charles went to help Pedro with Amy.

The girl was stirring, and the wound on her arm seemed to have stopped bleeding, but Pedro insisted on having a feather mattress carried down to the main room of the inn.

It was fortunately empty, and Pedro permitted the innkeeper's wife, a homely and sensible-looking woman, to cut away the sleeve of Amy's gown and attend to the wound.

'This elder-leaf wash be freshly made this morning,' she said as she worked. 'It cleans the wound, see. Girl, fetch me the crushed lavender, then make a brew of bergamot,' she added, and a child of about ten who was hovering nearby ran away to the kitchen.

A fragrant poultice of crushed lavender leaves was spread over the cut, which was fortunately not deep and had almost stopped bleeding. By the time a fresh strip of linen was bound round Amy's arm, she was conscious.

As she opened her eyes, she saw Pedro leaning over her, and smiled. Gently he laid his finger on her lips and spoke.

'Do not talk yet, my love. All is well, and I shall never again leave you.'

Amy nodded, permitted the innkeeper's wife to raise her while she obediently drank the tisane of bergamot, and soon afterwards was fast asleep.

Pedro reluctantly laid the hand he had been holding on the covers. He looked across at Bella and Charles.

'I should explain,' he said with a sigh, rising and crossing towards them.

'I think we understand,' Charles said. 'You never wanted to marry Bella.'

Pedro looked embarrassed.

'It was a family plan, made many years ago,' he said, sitting on a stool opposite them. 'I thought it would serve, but then I met Amy and we fell in love. I tried to forget her. I did not want to be in love, it interfered with plans made long ago. Thomas expected me to keep the promise made by my family. Then when the King began to show Bella his favour,

Thomas urged me to encourage a match. Until then my main thought had been how to prevent such a disaster, but Thomas saw it differently. He said the King could not live more than a year or two, long enough for Bella to get with child. He said I could still marry her after the King died, but by then I was so distraught at the thought of losing Amy I saw it only as a way out of my promise, an escape which would allow me to approach Amy with honour.'

'Honour!' Bella spluttered indignantly. 'You call it honourable to thrust me into the arms of that bloated monster!'

Pedro shrugged. 'I was so distraught, cousin. I did not consider you,' he said apologetically.

'How did you find us?' Bella asked.

'Thomas was summoned home by his wife, who heard from the village priest that old Lady Davenport had only a few days to live. He was too late. He came the day after she died. I came with him because I hoped to find Amy. We suspected you had run away together, though the King would have it that you had been abducted by a jealous rival who shared his own fascination for you.' Pedro grinned, and relaxed. 'Thomas was planning for me to play that part, I believe, and if the King was obdurate and refused to accept you back at Court, he would revive the notion of our marriage.'

'And you? What were your plans?' Charles asked.

'I do not know,' Pedro confessed. 'I thought I could forget Amy, yet I hoped to see her, especially after we heard that you had all left and it seemed you were heading for her home.'

'So you followed us there?'

'Yes. Two of the King's men had been left there to watch the house, but they were careless and did not see you. We discovered from the villagers her parents were in London, and you had been there but left again. It seemed likely you were making for London. We rode fast and caught up with your trail last night. We'd been following at a distance for an hour or more, but that was the first chance we had to do anything.'

'And now?' Bella asked softly.

'I cannot risk losing Amy again,' Pedro said simply. 'If she will forgive me, and her parents will accept me, I want to marry her. Bella, please understand.'

'And Thomas, if he deigns to return? Will he understand?' Bella demanded.

'That matters naught. He will need to go home to see to the disposition of his grandmother's estate. Jane was most reluctant to permit him to come with me.'

'I expect he will be halfway to Oxford by now,' Bella said scornfully.

'But what will you do? Shall I escort you back home?' Pedro offered.

Before Bella could begin her reply, Charles said, 'Bella is betrothed to me, and will come with me to France. We will hire more horses and travel together to Amy's sister's house, and then take our leave of you.'

## CHAPTER 9

An hour later, Amy awoke from her sleep ravenously hungry, and wondering whether she was dreaming that not only was Pedro there by her side, but he was declaring undying love for her.

Charles and Bella, feeling superfluous, left the room and sat outside on a bench underneath a large tree.

Bella sat quietly, her gaze pensive, and Charles, after a swift glance at her, remained silent. When they went back inside, Amy smiled mistily at them, holding tightly to Pedro's hand. Her arm was sore, but she declared she was quite capable of riding the rest of the way as soon as she had eaten.

The innkeeper's wife provided pies and ale, and afterwards, they set off. Charles had been out and hired another couple of horses, for the two they had could not carry double burdens for very far. By mid-afternoon they were once more riding towards London. Bella scarcely glanced about her, she was too deeply engrossed in her own problems.

Only when they had passed Smithfield and were riding through the narrow, crowded streets of the city did she begin to take notice of the scenes crowding in on them.

'It smells!' she exclaimed in disgust, wrinkling up her nose.

'It is partly the river, partly the Fleet ditch which is nearby, and because it is so hot,' Charles explained.

'Where does your sister live, Amy?' Bella asked her friend.

'Her husband is a goldsmith, they have a big house in Goldsmith's Row, in Cheape which runs near St Paul's.'

'Near the friends I had intended to stay with,' Charles commented. 'It will be convenient while I make arrangements for Bella and me to go to France.'

Bella glanced quickly at him. She had made no mention of leaving him, of refusing to marry him. It would be soon enough to start what she suspected would be a fierce argument when she had decided what she intended to do. At the moment she had not the slightest idea.

'I will visit this friend of mine, a merchant from Bordeaux, as soon as I have escorted you to Amy's house. He has lived here for many years. He will tell me all the news.'

'You do not mean to go back to Hampton Court Palace? What about your clothes, everything you left there?'

It was the first time Bella had even considered that in his headlong dash to rescue her he had abandoned all his possessions. Now he had only what he had purchased during the journey.

'I shall send a message to someone to pack them and send them to France. Do not worry, I always travel light. There is nothing irreplaceable.'

Recalling the expensive doublets and other clothes she had seen him wearing at Court, Bella was dubious, but she accepted this.

An amazing bustle ensued when the party arrived at Amy's sister's house. Servants were called to carry in the saddlebags while others took charge of the horses. Amy's mother, Lady Clifford, summoned from an upstairs room, fell upon her daughter with so many hugs and kisses and questions Amy did not have a chance to reply.

Eventually a tall, commanding man, slim, with an austere face and thick grey hair, appeared. Lady Clifford subsided, and Amy ran to greet her father.

'Come and eat, child. But first make me known to your friends.'

Sir Ralph Clifford's mere presence seemed to create order, and within seconds, it seemed they were seated in an upstairs room, plied with wine and small sweet cakes, and Charles was explaining the situation.

'You poor child!' Lady Clifford exclaimed to Bella. 'I am not surprised you ran away from such a fate!'

'That is understandable, but I do not see why you, Amy, must desert your mistress, the Lady Mary,' Sir Ralph said calmly.

Amy flushed. She could scarcely admit to an unhappy love affair when Pedro was there and planning to ask for her hand.

'I wished to give Bella some company and support,' she said slowly. 'I was not happy at Court, Father. It was so busy with intrigue and unseemly scrambling to obtain advancement or the royal favour.'

'I would not have thought your position high enough to be concerned with such matters,' he said mildly, and Amy flushed again and hung her head.

Lady Clifford broke in on the awkward silence.

'I am sorry about your grandmother, Bella. But it must have been a great comfort to her to have seen you before she died, and to know that you were now safe with the Comte de Nerac.'

Before Bella could think of how to announce that she did not intend to marry the Comte, Sir Ralph turned to him and began to question him about his plans for obtaining a passage to France.

'The ships are crowded. Many of your countrymen are leaving London.'

'Why is that? Is there more trouble?'

'The Emperor and Francis are once again at war. Now King Henry turns his attention to France in support of the Emperor. The English students in Paris are being recalled, and French merchants are being sent from England. Some troops have already been sent to Calais.'

'And the marriage between poor Lady Mary and the Duc d'Orleans is now unlikely,' Lady Clifford said. 'The King refused to give as big a dowry as King Francis wanted. Poor lady, she seems destined never to wed, unlike her father.'

'Why everyone should assume marriage to be such a desirable state, I cannot think!' Bella said later, when she and Charles were alone.

Charles chuckled. 'It presumably depends on the two people involved. Now you and I, my love—'

'Monsieur de Nerac, I am most grateful to you for all your help, but there is no need to continue the pretence. I have no wish to hold you to a promise made under duress.'

'There was no duress. I offered freely.'

'But I did not accept freely! I have no wish to marry you! I am not coming to France,' Bella said firmly.

He raised his eyebrows.

'Then what is your intention? To return to Hampton Court and the King's embraces? I suspect you would be unwelcome by now, my dear.'

'My plans are none of your concern!' she snapped. She dared not tell him she hadn't the faintest idea what she could do, and began to wish she had not been goaded into this argument.

To her relief, Lady Clifford and Amy then returned, and in high spirits Amy declared they were to go out at once and buy cloth to make gowns.

'You must replenish your wardrobes, immediately, or I will be heartily ashamed of you both,' Lady Clifford said cheerfully.

This was the opportunity she had waited for. She would be able to ask Lady Clifford's advice while they were out of the house, away from Charles. He took the opportunity to visit his French friends, a Monsieur Brossard and his wife.

Bella saw the sense of buying more clothes, even though they would not be her bridal attire. She had no wish to be a charge on Lady Clifford, however, and insisted on selling one of the smaller buckles from her grandmother's legacy in order to pay for her purchases.

To Bella's chagrin, both Amy and her mother were so absorbed in selecting silks and damask and fine woollen cloth, and discussing the designs of the gowns the girls needed, there was no opportunity for explaining her position to Lady Clifford.

In bed that night, she tossed and turned. Going home was out of the question. So was imposing on Lady Clifford, now that Amy was to be married. Amy seemed to have forgotten this plan in her joy at being reunited with Pedro, and Bella did not wish to spoil her happiness by reminding her of it. Besides, although she maintained an air of civility towards Pedro, she had no wish to have to live in the same house with him and Amy.

As she fell asleep just before dawn, Bella

had decided that her only choice was to go to her aunt's convent. She knew now that she could not bear to marry anyone but Charles. The convent life was not one she would have chosen, but her aunt had found contentment there, and perhaps she could, too.

The next morning Charles came back from the Brossard house with news.

'There is a boat leaving tomorrow, on the first tide. I have booked passages for us and the Brossards. We must be there by six in the morning, all of us. Soon, Bella, my love, you will be safely in France.'

And then, she thought, I can tell him I will not marry him...

The boat was small and crowded with Frenchmen and women returning to their native land, banished by King Henry because of his quarrel with Francis. There were no cabins, everyone having to find space where they could for sleeping.

The first part of the journey was uneventful as they sailed down the Thames and followed the Kent coastline.

'Two days, if we are fortunate with the winds,' Charles said cheerfully. 'When we reach France, would you like to go to Paris first? Perhaps be married there?'

Bella shook her head. The time had come to tell him the truth.

'You only made that foolish suggestion because Grandmother expected it of you. It's not what I want.'

'She did not ask me to do it, Bella. It was quite my own idea.'

'But she must have made her wishes clear. Charles, it was kind of you to say it and make her last hours contented, but I have no wish to hold you to it. I will marry only when I'm sure a man loves me for myself. I would hate to have any sense of obligation between myself and a husband.'

'Would it make any difference if I said I did love you?'

Her heart gave a leap of anticipation, then she shook her head. He was only being gallant. Besides, she told her rebellious heart, nothing he did now excused the fact he had tried to use her to spy on her mistress.

'You sought me out because I was one of Lady Mary's attendants,' she said coldly. 'I know the people on your embassy were trying to discover everything they could about her. I don't like spying.'

'Is that what you thought?' he asked in astonishment.

'Why else would you seek me out? There were many girls at Court prettier and more willing to flirt than I.'

'I wonder why you caught the eye of the King then?' he demanded angrily. 'I am no spy, and any questions I may have asked about your mistress were but attempts at polite conversation on an interest we had in common.'

Bella wanted to believe him, but a stubborn streak refused to let her. She shrugged, and turned to gaze over the rail of the ship at the white cliffs lining the coast. When she glanced back, Charles was conversing with several other young men on the other side of the ship. He did not return all the rest of the day.

When darkness fell Bella found herself a corner wedged between some of the packages the Brossards had brought with them, and tried to sleep.

By morning Bella was stiff and cold and her head ached. Charles, she saw, was some way off, but now he was talking animatedly with a delicately pretty, blonde girl whose smile was, even to Bella's prejudiced eye, enchanting.

She turned away and tried to ignore Madam Brossard's sly attempts to probe. Where were they on their journey? For a moment she felt some panic, for there was no land to be seen in any direction. Then she looked more carefully and realised there were several ships in the distance, gradually drawing nearer. Company would be welcome.

The wind seemed stronger, and the ship was rolling more. A few of the passengers were looking pale and apprehensive. Bella saw sailors scrambling about in the rigging and hoisting more sails. The ship was gathering speed, the sails billowing.

Monsieur Brossard looked worried, and

turned to a man on his far side.

'Why have we changed direction? We're heading eastwards, when surely France lies to the south?'

The other shrugged. 'I no longer know where I am or why!' he said angrily. 'I have lost my home and my ship, am being sent back to a country I left when I was but three years old, and all because our rulers want a little more power.'

Half an hour later, an incredulous Bella was hearing frightened rumours that the ships now rapidly overhauling them were English and threatening.

'They have been hunting French ships in the Channel for some time,' one well-informed man said.

At the same moment there was a bang, a whistling sound, and suddenly one of the sails was flapping wildly. Some of the ropes which tethered it to the mast had been severed by a lucky shot from a cannon. Bella could see a fine plume of smoke from one of the ships now openly pursuing them.

Many of the women screamed, and

children, affected by the panic, cried and whimpered. Sailors tried frantically to prevent the loose sail from collapsing on to the frightened passengers, but they were only partially successful. It collapsed like a giant sheet over part of the deck.

There were more screams as the people trapped fought wildly to escape its enveloping folds. Gradually the sailors managed to remove the sail.

There had been several more bangs, but with the confusion on board, little notice had been taken of them. The ship gave a fearful judder, and the boards creaked, splintering noises mingling with the general uproar.

'Bella? Good girl, stay calm.'

It was Charles, and Bella turned to cling to him.

'What is it? Who are they?' she demanded.

'It is the English. They are attacking the boat,' he replied calmly. 'They have scored one hit, but we are not very far from the coast.'

Bella stared at him in amazement. 'Will

we all drown?' she whispered.

'If we do not reach the coast quickly.'

The boat gave an odd little lurch. Bella stumbled and was thrown against Charles, who held her tightly.

'What was that?' she asked, looking up into his face and discovering that his eyes had remarkably long lashes for a man. What a stupid thing to notice, she chided herself, when in a few minutes she might be drowned.

'The boat is shipping water. But look over there. You can see land!'

Others had seen it, too, and gradually the panic gave way to hope.

The boat, shipping water fast, but with every sail hoisted, limped slowly across what seemed an endless stretch of water towards a low spur of land. Bella was conscious of a coolness in the air, and looking round saw the sun had set. The English boats, too near the coast of France, had drawn away.

As darkness fell, Bella stood and watched the coastline as long as it was visible, with Charles's arms about her, and his lips caressing her forehead. She didn't know that tears were falling slowly down her cheeks, for the cruel waste of the love she had to give him.

# CHAPTER 10

It seemed like hours before the lookout signalled from his post high in the rigging.

'Land ahoy!' he cried, and a great cheer went up from the passengers.

'How can he tell we are near?' Bella demanded, standing at the rail with Charles's arm about her waist.

'He will be able to see lights inland from that height,' Charles suggested, and he was right. A few minutes later, Bella saw for herself the faint glow from a building straight in front of them.

'Where is the shore? Can the ship reach land? How far away is it?' she demanded, straining to penetrate the enveloping darkness.

'Near enough to swim, I'm sure,' he replied cheerfully.

'I cannot swim!' Bella gasped in dismay.

'You can hold on to me. I will get us

both ashore.'

'Does the ship not have small boats? Surely that is one over there.'

'Only a couple of small ones, not enough for everyone. And there may not be time to launch them.'

Wordlessly she clung to the rail. She was sure the boat was listing heavily to one side, the deck sloping more than it had before.

'Come to the other side,' Charles said quietly, and Bella moved with him, grateful for the support of his arm over the steeply-sloping deck.

'Why?' she asked.

'If the boat goes suddenly, it will be that side first. We would be swept into the water by all these loose packages and the press of people. Here we can hold on to the rail and help ourselves more.'

The ship somehow limped on, and in the faint starlight Bella distinguished a darker ridge some way ahead.

'Is that the shore?' she asked.

'Yes, it must be. Not far away now.'

Hardly were the words uttered than the

ship struck something, and keeled over at a grotesque angle. Screaming passengers were thrown to the decks, and slid and rolled helplessly to fall into the seething waters below. If Charles had not been holding her in a grip of iron, Bella would have followed them.

Bella realised in some detached part of her mind that the moon, fortunately full, was rising far behind them and beginning to light up the scene. Several passengers had, like themselves, been able to cling to the rail or other solid parts of the ship, and some of them were crying out in panic, or calling for loved ones no longer with them.

'Come, we must move. Do exactly as I say,' Charles said softly.

He began to edge along the deck towards the stern, taking Bella with him. When he found a coil of rope, he used his dagger to hack away a length of it. He tied one end firmly round her waist, the other about himself, leaving a yard or so slack between them.

'I am not losing you now,' he said,

grinning at her puzzled look.

He found a rope ladder which dangled free from the side of the ship.

'That will make our descent easier to control,' he muttered, and he picked Bella up and swung her over the rail.

'I cannot!' she jerked out, but he was beside her instantly, and dropped a swift kiss on to her lips.

'Of course you can. I will be right behind you.'

He tested the ladder, which was firm, and eased himself on to it. Then he pulled Bella in front of him so that she was cradled between his arms.

'Hook your elbows over my arms, and hold the ladder above my hands. You cannot fall.'

Bella took a deep breath and firmly chastised herself. She was in a far better situation than the poor wretches who'd been flung into the water, whose cries she could hear below as they thrashed about amid the debris of the scattered packages and other items hurled with them from the decks.

Gradually she managed the descent, feeling with her feet for the rungs, and wishing she still retained her masculine attire. Some of the other passengers still on deck were trying to follow, while others loudly demanded help from the captain and his crew.

'Let go the rope now,' Charles said in her ear, and Bella instinctively obeyed him, only to wave her arms wildly in a desperate attempt to grasp it again as she felt herself falling backwards.

The water was very cold, and for a moment the shock made Bella gasp for breath. It covered her head, and she swallowed some water, then found herself choking and coughing as Charles held her in his arms.

'It is not far to the shore, and soon you'll be able to walk in the shallow water,' he told her. 'Go limp, do not struggle, and I will tow you along on your back. And keep your mouth closed this time.'

'I wish you had warned me before!' Bella said raggedly.

'I do not expect I will have many

opportunities to tell you to stop scolding me,' he murmured in her ear as he swiftly turned her round and grasped her under the armpits. 'Leave it all to me now.'

The next ten minutes were the most terrifying in Bella's life, and seemed more like ten hours. Utterly helpless, her skirts dragging at her legs, she found herself unable to see much apart from the crippled ship, or hear anything for the water which filled her ears. She was aware of others swimming beside them, and screams from farther away, and suddenly began to pray with desperate urgency that they would all be saved from a terrible death.

Suddenly the movement stopped, and she found Charles lifting her higher in the water.

'You can stand upright here, my love, and we can walk the rest of the way.'

And with one arm about her, he forced her to begin wading through the increasingly shallow water.

'What about all the others?' Bella asked as Charles struggled to undo the knots in the rope which had held them together.

'Some have swum ashore already, look,' he said, and she saw several men sprawled on the sand.

'The boats?'

'They launched one, and are picking up some of the passengers. Now stay here. I'm going to go back and see if I can help.'

A little while later, Bella noticed a pair of children clinging to a plank of wood, crying weakly. They were only a few yards offshore, and Bella immediately set off to try and reach them.

She waded out almost to her waist before she could seize the plank. The older child gave her a faint smile, and spoke in French.

'Take Louise. She has almost fallen off.'

'Hold tightly till I can get back!' Bella ordered. She grasped the younger child, lifting her high in her arms as she turned to wade back to shore.

A man who had seen what she was doing went past her.

'I will get the other one. They are building a fire. Get her there and warm.'

Bella turned and saw flames licking at a pile of wood which had somehow been gathered near the dunes. There were also the lights of lanterns, so presumably someone on shore had seen the wreck and come to help them.

At that moment a woman flung herself on Bella, and the child was lifted out of her arms, the two of them weeping and laughing with joy at being reunited.

'Maman, Maman!' the little girl wept, and Bella turned back to the water with a smile to see if there was anything else she could do.

'Bella!' She heard her name called and as it was repeated saw Charles wading out of the water with another child in his arms.

'Take this lad to the fire,' he said briskly, and Bella once more found herself carrying an exhausted child towards the welcoming warmth.

She waded into the sea several more times to help the people brought ashore by the boats or by those who could swim.

Most were exhausted, almost too weak

to stagger through the shallows, but they were helped by the stronger ones and taken to rest beside one of the many fires which had been lit.

Bella moved as if in a dream. She had had almost no sleep the previous night, had spent most of the day in terror, and several hours wading into the water and carrying children. When a sailor took her arm and led her towards one of the fires, she went unresisting.

Bella sank on to the sand, and dimly realised that the sun was rising. Her last thought before she fell asleep was that it would help to dry her clothes, and she needed help. She was cold, so very cold.

Seconds later she found herself being carried in strong arms. Hazily she opened her eyes and found that in some strange fashion the sun was high overhead. But she was still cold, and her wet clothes clung stickily to her body.

'Charles?' she murmured, and he answered immediately.

'I am going to find somewhere and make you dry and warm again.'

She looked about her. He had left the dunes behind, and was striding across what seemed to be open heathland. She drifted back into an uneasy sleep.

When next she woke it was because Charles had stripped off her gown and was struggling with the tapes of her petticoats.

'What are you doing?' she asked.

'Trying to get you dry,' he replied briskly.

'But where are we?'

'At the side of a haystack.'

'A haystack!'

He laughed, and gave a final tug at her petticoats.

'Warm, soft, dry, something to rub life back into us, and cover us when we are ready to sleep. It even smells good.'

Bella sniffed appreciatively. It was true. There was a tantalising mixture of sun-dried herbs amongst the hay! Then she realised she was almost naked and hastily clutched her shift about her.

Charles laughed. 'I'll spare your modesty while I get out of my own wet clothes. Take off every last stitch of clothing, spread it out to dry, and then rub yourself dry with some hay. You can bury yourself in it afterwards.'

It felt decidedly strange to be wandering around naked on the edge of a haystack finding suitable places for laying out her clothes, then sitting in the warm sun, scrubbing at her body as if she were a horse being groomed. The thought crossed her mind that Charles could be rubbing her down if she were a horse, and a deep crimson tide of embarrassment swept over her whole body.

Pausing only to push her belt containing the jewels into the hay beneath her, she made frantic haste to bury herself deep in the loose hay. Then she pulled more down on top of her until only her face was visible.

Some time later her dream disturbed her and Bella woke with a scream.

'Hush, my love, you're safe now,' Charles said soothingly, his arms about her. 'Go back to sleep, my love. It will be dawn in an hour or so, and then we can plan how to continue our journey.'

Still exhausted, but warm and comfortable, Bella forgot everything else in her need for sleep. It was long past dawn when she woke again and, with sleepy recollection, stretched out her hand towards Charles. He had gone.

'Charles?' she called softly.

'Bella? You're awake at last!'

He appeared round the side of the haystack, his clothes streaked with the seawater and stiff with salt. The sight made her aware of her own lack of clothes, and she hastily buried herself more deeply in the hay.

'When you are dressed, we will go in search of breakfast,' he said calmly. 'Your clothes are all dry.'

He dropped a bundle on top of her, and chuckled as he turned away. Bella fastened on her belt with the jewels and struggled into her clothes, finding them in no better state than his.

Their walk across fields to the small village some way inland was silent. Bella was embarrassed still by her memory of sleeping in Charles's arms during the night, and he did not appear to wish to talk. In the village they were greeted eagerly, and taken into the huge kitchen of a large farmhouse where they were plied with bread and cold meats. They found themselves in the company of a dozen more survivors of the wreck.

Afterwards, Charles, who had been talking to some of the other people, came back to her.

'We need to talk,' he said abruptly.

Bella rose and followed him out of the kitchen, into a small orchard where the trees were laden with apples.

'When you were dreaming, you were trying to fight me off, crying that you would not marry me,' he said slowly. 'Is that what you really want?'

'You offered to please Grandmother,' Bella replied quietly. 'I do not wish to hold you to a promise you might one day regret.'

'If you really mean it, why did you come with me to France?'

'I meant to go to Bordeaux, to my aunt.'

'Bella, you are not meant to be a nun. You are a beautiful, vital woman, meant for loving. No, listen to me. I will have my say and then you may make your decision. If you choose to go to Bordeaux there are people here who would be happy for you to join their party and travel with them. I will make no objection, but I hope you will choose to stay with me. Can you not bring yourself to try to love me?'

'But you cannot mean it! You offered to please Grandmama!'

'I offered to please myself, and you, too, I hoped. I flattered myself I would be a more acceptable bridegroom than King Henry. I hoped that even if you did not love me, then you might come to do so. I became utterly ensnared the moment I set eyes on you in the Great Hall, and have since then thought of little but how I might make you my wife, make you love me, spend the rest of my life pleasing you, caring for you, cherishing you. But I will not constrain you against your own wishes. If you cannot bear the thought of marriage to me then I will regret it all my days, but never blame you.'

Bella stared at him, deeply moved by his sincerity and finally convinced he did love her. She could now admit her own love.

'I thought you did not love me,' she whispered softly. 'I could not bear it if you married me as a duty, or because of a promise. I loved you so much I could not become a burden, causing you to do something you might regret.'

For a few incredulous moments, Charles stared at her, then he swept her into his arms and kissed her until she was laughingly begging for mercy.

'Shall we go to Paris and marry there, or wait until we reach my home?' he asked, breathless.

'Is there not a priest here? Once the passengers have gone their ways, might he have time to marry us? After all, what would people think if we were to travel alone, and were not married?'

'They would undoubtedly be shocked, and it might be a little difficult to acquire boy's clothing for you! You are sure, my love?'

'Yes.' She sighed contentedly. 'I was sure a long time ago, but I could not bear it if you were not.'

'I shall spend the rest of my life proving to you how much I adore you, my lovely Bella,' he said huskily, and took her in his arms once more to kiss her in a manner which left her in no doubt as to the truth of his words.

This Large Print Book for the Partially sighted, who cannot read normal print, is published under the auspices of

## THE ULVERSCROFT FOUNDATION

---

## THE ULVERSCROFT FOUNDATION

. . . we hope that you have enjoyed this Large Print Book. Please think for a moment about those people who have worse eyesight problems than you . . . and are unable to even read or enjoy Large Print, without great difficulty.

You can help them by sending a donation, large or small to:

**The Ulverscroft Foundation,
1, The Green, Bradgate Road,
Anstey, Leicestershire, LE7 7FU,
England.**

or request a copy of our brochure for more details.

The Foundation will use all your help to assist those people who are handicapped by various sight problems and need special attention.

Thank you very much for your help.